CW00863474

The Chronicles of Captain Colin

AP Whitmore

Illustrations by Carley French

authorHOUSE®

AuthorHouse™ UK Ltd.
500 Avebury Boulevard
Central Milton Keynes, MK9 2BE
www.authorhouse.co.uk
Phone: 08001974150

This book is a work of fiction. People, places, events, and situations are the product of the author's imagination. Any resemblance to actual persons, living or dead, or historical events, is purely coincidental.

First published by AuthorHouse 10/19/2009

ISBN: 978-1-4490-1202-1 (sc)

This book is printed on acid-free paper.

For Colin Frederick Whitmore – a wonderful dad:
Captain Colin is flying for you

Contents

Preface

Dear Reader

I first met Captain Colin when I was out walking one grey afternoon in the summer of 2007. I was minding my own business when he knocked on the door of my thoughts, came in without so much as a 'by your leave', settled down and has been there ever since.

Every story has a challenge and this one is no different. Captain Colin nearly didn't make it to the printed page but he stayed firmly in my mind, tickling my conscience, demanding to be written. I resisted for about a year, too busy with other things. However, the feeling that I absolutely must tell his story grew too great to ignore. In the end I listened and I am so glad that I did.

Together we built up his character; father and resident hero; a kind man with time for everyone but tough and fearless when the need arises. His adventures take him across the sea, into battle with magical characters and always bring him home to his family and his project, the lunar rocket.

I hope you enjoy reading his story as much as I enjoyed writing it.

AP Whitmore

Acknowledgments

My grateful thanks to Carley French for bringing the book to life with her wonderful illustrations.

My grateful thanks to Sarah Shervington for her rigorous and comprehensive editing.

My special thanks to Pat and Ali Whitmore, Mark Moore, Helen Gerlach, Helen Keedwell, Paul Wiscombe, Claire Browne and the children from the Topsham School, Marian Weston, Brent Davison, Linda Rayner, Nicky Barwick, Sally Blades, Liz Scott, Sarah Grace Cordell and Belinda Goodman for their feedback, support and belief that Captain Colin deserved a story of his own.

PROLOGUE: IN WHICH WE MEET OUR HERO

Many years ago a young married couple, pregnant with their first baby, went to see a clairvoyant, Chlorenia, who lived on the edge of the City. Such magic practices were well regulated and tolerated.

The clairvoyant was a very ordinary looking person, dressed in a long brown cloak and with a funny idea of customer service.

She took their money and then barked a series of questions at the couple, without looking at them.

'Names?'

'Cyril and Florence.'

'Occupations?'

'Coach driver and housewife.'

The clairvoyant then turned to a giant electric abacus and started to type in an impossibly long and complicated mathematical formula on a small keypad at its base. There was silence for a minute and then a ribbon shot out of the side of the machine, punctuated by small holes.

The clairvoyant ran her fingers along the ribbon, muttering as she did so. Next she rolled her eyes and her head fell back, so you could see right up her nose. Then, facing the anxious couple once more, she said,

'The baby is a boy so fair,
Traveller, pilot in the air,
Hero, lover of fine food
And fighter for the common good.
But in his heart he has a hole.
To plug it will be his life's goal.
Only when ten travails have ended,
Will his heart be truly mended.'

Then she went into a trance and the couple, scared and a little confused, slipped out of the cottage and drove back towards the City.

'She was strange,' said Florence, relieved to be gone.

Cyril shook his head. 'What was all that muttering about? And that poetry?'

'I wrote it down,' Florence admitted and then put her hands on her stomach with a smile. 'I think he is going to be a rugby player.'

Cyril grinned in the dark. 'Grand.'

And so it was that their little boy - their only child - was born.

Captain Colin was a hero of our times. In his stockinged feet he stood taller than any pygmy, shorter than any giant and shoulder to shoulder with any other man.

He was a leader of people, a slayer of dragons (small and medium sized) and a righter of wrongs. No wrong was too wrong to be righted.

As he led his team in the Justiciary, fearlessly doing battle with the criminal underworld, the sun glinted off his rubicund (this is an extra special version of rosy) cheeks and the twinkle in his eye belied a fierce pride in his work. The Justiciary is a bit like a police service and customs office all rolled into one.

The City he guarded was a city state – that means that it was independent. It had its own city council, chaired by Mayor Chillblain, which passed the laws that the people lived by.

The City had trading links with other such cities, which formed the Federation of Homeland Cities, or FHC for short. Trade was regulated and monitored to make sure that people in the City had as much access to high quality goods as possible, such as organically grown food or wooden products from sustainable sources.

The City's people were honest, hardworking folk in the main, with a few scoundrels and scallywags to keep the Justiciary on its toes. Some of these people, like Mayor Chillblain and Witch Warble will meet you later on in the story.

The City was a pleasant, green place, smaller than London, but bigger than Bath. It had schools and universities, shops and factories, businesses and houses, parks and hospitals; in fact everything you would expect to see in your town.

Captain Colin knew every nook and cranny of its streets and alleys. He had grown up there, met his wife, Mary, while training as an agent in the Justiciary Academy, where she was also working as a trainer. They lived in a large rambling house on the city outskirts, where their three children roamed around. The children, two girls and a boy, were called Alison, Beatrice and Christopher. They all went to school in the City and had lots of friends there.

They knew that their Dad did an important job, that he sometimes worked long hours, that he sometimes got cramp when he was very tired and that, on very rare occasions, he got cross. But to them he was the best Dad in the world.

Since you are a very clever reader you may have already guessed that magic plays a small part in these stories. Naughty dragons and unscrupulous dentists were part of life in the City and Captain Colin and his crack team (including the agents of Candy Command) knew how to deal with them.

But Captain Colin had a secret – a flaw that no naked eye could see. He kept this secret so well hidden that, a lot of the time, even he forgot it was there. Nevertheless, sometimes the sun lights up even the darkest corners and makes us remember what we would rather forget.

This secret was not a vice, or a sin committed and never admitted. It was not a character flaw or a terrible habit. It was not a lie. It was simply that Captain Colin's heart was incomplete.

He loved his family and his work but that was not enough. His heart was still under construction. He had tinkered with the edges, screwing in a rivet here and a bolt there. But he had not yet experienced it in its entirety, with the engine at full throttle, the world below him like a vast shining map.

All the pieces were there and had been carried from one location to another in a trailer, in the form of a lunar rocket, ready to be assembled, ready to set him free. When completed, it would be a like a magnificent metal tube, powering through the sky, gleaming from tip to tip.

Until Captain Colin chose the moment to fly his lunar rocket, he kept his feet on the ground, with a smile on his lips and the sword of justice in his hand. There were some very frightened small and medium sized dragons on the run!

How Captain Colin completed his heart is the subject of these chronicles.

Travail One: The
Shadow Stealer

O ne morning, in late summer, Miss Jolly left her house at eight on the dot, to go to work. It was a short walk, which her shadow always took with her, rippling over buildings, pavement edges and merging in with other shadows on the way.

At one o clock, Miss Jolly met her friends for lunch in the park. Sitting on the bench, enjoying a fizzy drink and some fruit, she felt like she didn't have a care in the world. It was only when she got up to go that she felt a shiver go down her spine. Something was wrong. She looked around her. Her purse was in her bag and all her litter in the bin. She hadn't left anything behind.

The feeling persisted as she walked back across the grass towards the office building. What was it? Suddenly it came to her. Everyone was walking round with the one thing she no longer had.

Her shadow had been stolen!

At about the same time as Miss Jolly left for work, a teenager listening to some trance music was hatching a plan. Herbert Garden, known to his friends as Herb, was completely fed up.

At fifteen, his voice was jumping about all over the place, he had broken out in spots and his hands and feet seemed to be growing at a speed all of their own. Recently he had plucked up the courage to ask a girl out at school. It had taken all his nerve and he had stood waiting for her answer, his palms sweating and his heart thumping.

'What – me go out with you? I don't think so?' She had turned back to her friends and they had spent the rest of the break giggling behind their hands and looking at him, which had really upset him.

Hot with shame and determined to get revenge, Herb's plan was simple. As a black belt level player of the Fandango XM game 'The Shadow Stealer', he had used his skill to make a shadow proof sack, rope and gloves. He would steal a female shadow, use it as a decoy, get into the girls' changing rooms unseen while it was empty, fill their trainers with mud and make them sorry they had ever laughed at him. He would laugh as they squelched round, imagining their cries of horror and disgust.

In the park at lunch time Herb loitered, his earphones on, watching behind his sunglasses. He spotted Miss Jolly, with her back to her shadow, catching some rays and not paying attention.

Shadows can't shout and, as Herb grabbed it, it tussled with him, looking like a heroine in a silent film, shaking its head and flailing its arms, but finally overpowered and pushed into the sack, the inside of which was covered with shadow proofer. This meant that the shadow could be tied up and not escape, as it was coated with a special goo. Then Herb sauntered away, ready to put the next phase of his plan into operation.

Just after that, on the same day, Captain Colin was going about his business in his usual, fearless way. It was a busy day with lots of little things to do. When his mobile telephonic device sounded, he picked it up and spoke into the mouthpiece.

'This is Captain Colin. How might I be of service?'

There was a pause and then a frightened voice said, 'My shadow is missing.'

Captain Colin stopped what he was doing and grabbed a pen and paper. 'Take your time, tell me who you are and what has happened.'

The caller, who sounded young and nervous, took a deep breath. 'My name is Fleur Jolly and someone appears to have stolen my shadow.'

The Captain sucked in his breath. This was a serious crime indeed and cases were tricky to handle. They had to be investigated in broad daylight, which meant undercover work for the agents involved. A shadow stealer could pretend to be somebody else in daylight (though not at night), by using someone else's shadow to hide their own. Herb could use Miss Jolly's shadow, so that anyone looking into the changing rooms while he was there would see a female shadow and not worry. This would provide the perfect cover for him to carry out his horrid trick. It was tantamount to identity theft.

Captain Colin thought on his feet. 'You need to make your way to the Justiciary and speak to one of our experts.'

'I will do that straight away,' promised Miss Jolly, her voice a bit less shaky. She set off immediately.

In an office at the back of the Justiciary, Special Agent Crispy had set up and was waiting for Miss Jolly. Captain Colin joined them – cases like this needed the finest agents there were.

Miss Jolly gave her personal details, took a sip of her water and the interview began.

'Can you describe your shadow to me?' asked Agent Crispy.

'Yes – it's about five foot six tall and one foot wide. It is shorter at noon and longer in the evenings and looks, I suppose, like me in outline.' Miss Jolly was comforted by Captain Colin's assured air and Agent Crispy's perspicacious questioning.

She was indeed five foot six tall and one foot wide, although her height didn't fluctuate between midday and evening. Despite being in such safe hands she was very nervous and agitated and kept looking around her, as if she had lost something.

A shadow was a bit like that. It was one of those things that you didn't realise you would miss until it wasn't there any longer. That was precisely what Miss Jolly was experiencing and she didn't like it one bit.

'Right, now that we have got your shadow's likeness, we can do a scan for an s-fit, issue a bulletin to all agents and have you reunited in a jiffy.' Agent Crispy smiled as he handed the document to Agent Crunchy, who had just popped her head round the door. She was the best scanner in the business.

The shadow scan was taken and the resulting three part s-fit so lifelike that when she saw it, Miss Jolly gasped, looking at Agent Crunchy with considerable admiration.

Miss Jolly then looked across at Captain Colin and his smile comforted her and the sun shone off his teeth.

'What happens now?' she asked, partly because she wanted to know and partly because her admiration for the Captain and his agents had pinned her to her chair.

He smiled again, in his reassuring way. 'Now we get to work. You might have to wait a while, I'm afraid. Agent Crispy will show you where you can sit and have a cup of tea and a biscuit.'

Agent Crunchy had been busy and pretty soon the s-fit had been circulated to all relevant agents and a briefing was held. Special equipment was issued, including anti-shadow sunglasses (which made them easier to spot), shadow proof gloves for easy handling and a shadow proof sack, to stop a captured shadow from slipping out before it could be returned to its owner.

Then, unseen, four or five figures slipped out of the building and became lost in the crowds of people in the streets.

Barely an hour had gone by when a call came in from an agent in the west sector of the City. The message 'female shadow in distressed state' was radioed in.

Herb was hot and tired. Carrying a squirming shadow around was hard work in the summer heat. Shadows didn't weigh very much, but this one wriggled non-stop. Seeing Morts, a famous sweetshop in this area, he dumped the sack, let the shadow out and tied it to a post.

'Don't move or I will zap you,' he threatened and ducked inside to get some sweets.

Agents had spotted the shadow without an owner tied to a post outside the sweet shop. It matched the description of the stolen shadow, but the agents needed to proceed with caution. The shadow was holding it hands up, clearly distressed. The agents looked at each other with grim faces. Whoever the thief was, they knew their stuff – that shadow had been proofed so it could be tied up!

This was delicate work and the agents took up their positions on opposite sides of the street, using their radios on a special frequency and speaking to one another in a special radio code, using letters of the alphabet. It went something like this.

Agent A: C (I have the shadow in view)

Agent B: OK (I understand and await your further update)

Agent A: V.R.O.K. (Go on my next signal)

These agents learned many skills to equip them to do their job well and they were using a special code called squeakwave. It used technology cleverly to scramble the agents' conversation into a sort of high pitched drone, which meant it couldn't be decoded by unscrupulous eavesdroppers.

A young teenaged lad emerged from the shop with the biggest bag of sweets the agents had ever seen and, walking towards the shadow, began to untie it. His own shadow was walking jauntily beside him.

'Come on, you,' Herb said harshly to the crying shadow. 'When I've used you, then I'll let you go, so stop your snivelling – we've got places to go and babes to see.'

There was another radio exchange between the agents.

Agent A: F.U.I? (Can you see them?)

Agent B: I.F.I. (Yes) V.R.Go! (Go, go, go!)

At exactly the same time the agents made a stealthy approach from the left and the right, in a pincer movement. Wearing all their protective equipment, they crept up on the unsuspecting adolescent, who was too busy searching out some milk chews to suspect an ambush. Agent A pointed at her sack and at Herb and Agent B nodded, pointing at his sack and Miss Jolly's shadow. They began to do a sort of fast creeping, knees bent, sacks at the ready.

Then disaster struck. Agent A, who was paying attention to her quarry and not the pavement, tripped on an uneven paving slab.

Racing forward to try and stop herself from falling, she kept her head raised and her arms holding the sack out in front of her in an effort to keep her balance. She cannoned off another passerby and, just as Herb turned to see what all the noise was about, threw her sack over him and they both collapsed to the ground.

Agent B looked on horrified, then came to his senses and ran towards the shadow.

The shadow, nervous and unsure, was pulling at the post and about to make a run for it, when Agent B spoke.

'We are city agents,' he said, 'and we are here to take you to the Justiciary and reunite you with your owner.'

The shadow tipped its head on one side, to show that it was listening, before holding out its hands palms up. 'OK,' it seemed to be saying, 'I trust you.'

The agents looked at Herb. He did look funny! The sack covered his head and shoulders and had been pulled tight at his elbows to stop him from running away. He made a sort of howling sound from inside the sack, but it

7

was ignored. Instead, Agent A, still a bit shaken inwardly from her near miss, had her hand on his elbow and was guiding him towards the vehicle.

Back at the Justiciary there was lots of activity. Miss Jolly had been informed that her shadow was well, an interview room was prepared and they awaited the arrival of the agents. The shadow was de-proofed and treated for minor shock.

A reunion with one's shadow is best done in the sunlight. Miss Jolly made a hugging gesture towards her shadow, as it stood there, irresolute and a little afraid.

'I missed you,' she said, 'and I am sorry.'

The shadow perked up at her words and made the same hugging gesture back, before snapping into place. The sense of relief was palpable and Miss Jolly thanked Captain Colin and his team prettily before going on her way

Herb looked around him at the room. This would make quite a story – he could imagine telling a group of adoring listeners about how he outsmarted the agents in their questioning. It was at this moment that Captain Colin and Agent A entered the room. Herb gulped behind his sneer. Captain Colin's reputation preceded him - even Herb knew who he was.

His strategy was to refuse to admit anything, despite being caught red handed. So he just bit his nails and scratched his ear.

Having confirmed who he was and where he lived with only a sullen nod, Captain Colin asked, 'What made you so upset, Herbert, that you would think about committing such a crime?'

Herb blinked and tried to resist the kind eyes and voice. He opened his mouth to say, 'Whatever.' But what came out, in a high pitched note followed by a deep rumbling one was, 'You try being me.'

Some careful questions and compassionate noises made Herb feel that they were really listening to him and slowly his story emerged; he told them about asking the girl out and her response. He described how, like, hurt he had been and how he was fed up of being the butt of their jokes. So, in anger, he had stolen a female shadow so that he could get into the girls' changing rooms at school while the shadow kept watch, fill their trainers with mud and, in his mind, maybe gain the upper hand through his prank.

Captain Colin looked at him sternly. 'Do you understand that this is wrong?'

The young lad raised his eyes and looked into the face of our hero. 'It's easy for you. <u>You</u> are a hero. I never get the girl. I'm not sporty, just spotty. My parents always told me I wouldn't amount to much and I wanted to show them that they were wrong.'

'By stealing?' Agent A asked in a hard voice.

Herb looked crestfallen. 'I've even messed this up.'

Captain Colin and Agent A had left the room to give Herb time to reflect on his behaviour. He was staring moodily at the table, his street cred in smithereens.

Agent A spoke first. 'It's clear to me that this boy has been the victim of a crime of sorts. He's had his self confidence drained out of him.'

'So, in return, he has tried to become someone else by stealing their shadow,' Captain Colin finished.

Having jointly agreed how to proceed, they went back into the room and Herb, despite trying to slouch in his seat and look like he didn't care, sat up straight. They looked like they meant business.

Captain Colin cleared his throat.

'Firstly, you will write a letter of apology to Miss Jolly for the inconvenience you have caused her. Secondly, you will do 50 hours of community service for the crime that you have committed. This will involve cutting hedges, weeding gardens and doing shopping for housebound citizens. Furthermore you will be served with an Anti-Shadow Burglary Order (ASBO). This will be in place for two years; until such time as you can prove that you have no further intention of doing such a thing again. Agent A will take you through to reception in a minute.'

He stopped and Herb winced. This was tough. He was going to have an ASBO. Then Captain Colin spoke again.

'However, we both agree that you have some considerable talents and you need some encouragement to develop them in more constructive ways.'

He paused and smiled. 'Have you heard of the Captain Colin Soccer Academy?'

Herb swallowed and nodded.

'Well, you will be offered membership and in return, you will be asked to design a website for the academy, as well as train with the squad. A word of warning, however; this is conditional on you completing your 50 hours with no trouble. Do I make myself clear?'

'Like, totally,' said Herb, who felt like he had just hitched a lift on a dream train, where wishes come true. 'Like, yes, I promise.'

So Herb wrote the letter of apology to Miss Jolly, which he was to deliver personally with Agent B (the first of his 50 hours) and went home with just the one shadow.

Later in the Justiciary foyer Agent A turned to Captain Colin and asked, 'Do you think that giving him a place at your academy could be seen as condoning his behaviour?'

He looked her in the eye, smiled in his wise way and said, 'Perhaps. He will have to work harder than he has ever worked in his life to show himself worthy of a place on the team. But it will build his self esteem so that he won't need anyone else's shadow to hide behind in the future.'

Agent A smiled. 'You can tell that you have children of your own to have dealt with this so wisely. I learn such a lot from working with you'

Captain Colin thought of his three lovely children and the engine of his heart revved. 'I am indeed a father and proud to be so.'

Then he remembered all the work left to do. 'Right, no more chat. There is work to be done and there are people to be saved. You're shaping up to be a very good agent, A.'

She blushed and muttered something that sounded like, 'O-you're-just-saying-that,' before disappearing to her office.

Much later that evening, in the shed with the bits of his heart all around him, Captain Colin thought about his children and all that they meant to him. Had anyone stolen their shadows, he would have pursued them to the ends of the earth, using any means.

And thus the first piece of his heart fell into place.

TRAVAIL TWO: THE LAUGHING GAS GANG

Summer had turned into Autumn and the trees were loaded with multicoloured leaves. The days were shorter and the autumnal mellowness belied a melancholy atmosphere at the onset of winter.

Under that gentle sky, a very ungentle plan was being hatched.

In a dilapidated warehouse in the very eastern sector of the City, eight men and women in white coats with badges bearing their names in black lettering were seated at a round table. Each had a paper in front of them, with some incredibly complicated arrows and writing on it. They were poring over this document as though it contained instructions to some great treasure; and in a way, it did!

Elsewhere, at precisely the same moment, a shopkeeper called Mort was going about his business. His shop was like a grotto, with glass jars full of the most delicious and rainbow coloured sweets. Under his front counter, open boxes full of chewy, tongue sizzling, teeth crunching goodies invited customers to buy the biggest bag possible and munch all the way home.

Morts was part of city folklore. For as long as any of the children or their parents could remember, there had been a sweet shop in that place. Every day, after school, gaggles of children crowded its narrow confines, chattering and choosing, then paying and swapping sweets outside.

The collection of men and women in white overalls had stopped looking at the paper and were listening in earnest to one of the women, as she outlined what seemed to be a plan.

'We will strike here,' Emilie Mola said, indicating a building on an aerial map. 'The gang on the ground are ready to move. They will get what they can and bring it back here. They have laughing gas to deal with the shopkeeper and are on standby for our signal. Shall we do it?'

One of the group, a younger woman called Gloria Incisor, raised her hand.

'Yes?' Emilie said impatiently.

'I can't help thinking that this goes against the Orthodontic Oath.' (This is what all dentists swear upon when they graduate and it gives them some rules for behaving well when they work). 'We all swore on that oath and, well, I have to say this doesn't feel right.' Gloria's voice shook.'We have been dentists in the City for generations.'

'Gloria, Gloria,' said the older woman. 'We are not working against the oath. We will treat all those children and adults who come to us with dental problems. We won't charge any more than we do now. We are just...well, just helping them to eat the sweets they want, so that we can treat the patients we want, only more of them.'

There was laughter from the others. It was to be an eventful and profitable day.

Through the streets of the City, a siren could be heard and any citizen would have recognised the driver at the helm of the vehicle. His face was stern and the desire to dispense justice was etched into every line of his face. Captain Colin was a man on a mission.

Earlier the same day a report had come in from a shopkeeper - Mort. The call handler taking the call had been unable to decode what the shopkeeper was saying, because he was laughing so hard. In the background was cackling and high pitched laughter and the distinct sound of lids being taken off jars and paper bags being rustled.

Further analysis of the recording of the call picked up something being sprayed, and each squirt was followed by what sounded like a pack of hyenas at a joke telling convention.

When Captain Colin and his crew arrived at the scene, the seriousness of what had occurred became only too evident. There were wrappers, jars, upturned boxes and bags strewn everywhere. The air was thick with a layer of icing sugar. All the sweets, chocolates, biscuits and cakes were gone and Mort – well Mort was doubled up somewhere between extreme stomach ache and laughter. And just behind him, on the counter, was a green canister, empty.

Laughing gas.

The Laughing Gas Gang were back in town; so called because they used laughing gas to render their victims helpless while they stole goods that did not belong to them.

This same gang had tormented the City for three months last year, leaving one poor victim traumatised because he had laughed so hard his hair had come off - literally. No one had realised it was a toupee.

The haul was extensive, including 50 packets of custard creems, 20 bars of milk chocolate and a lorry load of pear drops. On the candy market (illicit selling of sweet products – a thriving alternative economy which made these dentists rich!) this would fetch a pretty price. Captain Colin felt that somewhere out there an unscrupulous dentist cartel was at work.

'There's no fire without dragon,' he muttered, quoting a favourite motto of dragon slayers the galaxy over. 'This has the Laughing Gas Gang all over it.'

Back in the warehouse, the first report had just come in. The gang members were on their way and the dentists were itching to see what they had got. When the vehicles arrived (small, square, unobtrusive box cars) unloading began. The goods were divided up and readied for immediate export to different parts of the City.

Each dentist had a network of sweet touts, who hung around schools and play areas, infiltrating tuck shops and brownie/scout groups. They would target parents worn down by incessant demand for sweets, who would buy anything at any price to keep the peace. Nothing was ever traced back to the dentists. They appeared to be like their lab coats – cleaner than clean!

Mort, exhausted from all his laughing, was slumped over the cash till. Agents had been trying in vain to get some answers to their questions.

'Mr Mort, can you tell us how many people there were?'

'Hoo hoo ha ha hee hee hee ha ha hoo hoo,' chortled Mort.

The agent tried again. 'Do you have any security footage that we can look at?'

'Haaa haaaa heee heeee hooo hoooo ha ha hee hee ha ha,' laughed Mort, even louder and now very out of breath. He could only point at the security camera that had been installed. There was no film in it, but slung over the lens was a mask, taken off by one of the gang in the middle of doing the dastardly deed.

The item was bagged, along with the empty canister and sent to a crack candy forensic team straight away. Captain Colin drew himself up to his full taller than any pygmy height and looked the now exhausted shopkeeper in the eye.

'We may not retrieve your goods, Mr Mort, but we will restore your dignity,' he said.

'Thank you hoo hoo hee hee', gasped the poor man, now in need of sleep and wiping his eyes. 'Ha ha ha ha hee hee.'

Captain Colin strode back to his vehicle and, taking out his mobile telephonic device, spoke into the mouthpiece. He wanted the results from the mask and canister on his arrival back at the Justiciary and a crack team of competent pretenders assembled.

These were agents who infiltrated gangs, posing as customers. They were very good at what they did.

They were ready and waiting on his return; young, eager and ready to help resolve the biggest mystery of the modern era. Captain Colin strode into the room and looked round at them all. He briefed them succinctly and clearly, the look in his eye telling them that they must not fail him.

'Today the Laughing Gas Gang has struck again, cleaning out Morts completely.'

There was a gasp. Cleaning out Morts was like the ultimate act of disrespect. It was unthinkable.

Captain Colin nodded. 'Thousands of items have been taken and you know, as well as I do, what will happen. More sweets mean poor teeth, which mean more fillings. And somewhere in the midst of all of this, people that we trust are taking advantage of each and every one of us.'

He paused. 'The teeth of young and old alike depend on you. Everywhere where there is a dentist taking unfair advantage of illegal access to sweets, there you must be, like avenging angels, for healthy gums and the restoration of justice.'

Several minutes of briefing followed, which can't be revealed here as it is top secret. Then the agents filed out. Serious and thoughtful, each was determined to do their bit. Infiltrating the candy market was tough and dangerous and required stock worth trading.

FairlyTraded dark chocolate, hobbly nobbly biscuits with raisins AND curl wurl sticks were placed reverently in sacks for each agent and a cover story - so sound that it was unsinkable - was concocted. With the treasure in their sacks, they went out into the deepening gloom of the autumn evening.

Captain Colin would lead Candy Command – escalated to dark chocolate level (more serious even than rich tea level). As he waited, the first calls began to come in.

An anonymous caller reported that there was a glut of dairy milk bars, provenance unknown, fetching twice the normal price. Desperate parents stalked the alleyways, looking for ways to bribe their children into behaving well. A tout was doing a roaring trade in the north of the City.

Other calls followed. There had been scenes of chaos as parents and children alike, fooled into thinking there was a national shortage of chocolate buttons, scrambled to buy some in the city centre. Similar reports emerged all over the City, with footage of two boys having a tug of war over a liquorice string, which just got longer and longer the more they pulled.

Then the first breakthrough – one of the agents, Pindy, overheard a chance conversation between a tout on a radiophonic device and some kind of central command. It happened so quickly that he was lucky to have caught it.

The tout kept turning his head to the left, hunching his left shoulder and speaking into his collar. As the agent got closer, undetected, he could hear the following words, being repeated.

'Sell out imminent. Repeat, sell out imminent. Will leave in five and return to base. Sell out imminent. Will leave in five and return to base.'

With a careful look around, the tout disappeared, leaving the crowds to disperse. Agent Pindy followed, at a distance and out of sight, tracking him through a series of winding, narrow streets, where romantic tall houses accommodated artists, writers and celebrities.

On they went, one leading, the other following, until they came to an industrial park, with some very anonymous looking warehouse units, all locked for the night. The tout made a beeline for one at the back of site, near some fencing and slipped in through a side door. Agent Pindy paused only to give his location and request Candy Command back up, then slipped into the same building.

It was dark, almost pitch black and he turned down his radio, to avoid being discovered. A strange noise could be heard coming down a flight of iron steps; steps you might see in a factory. He climbed gingerly and carefully, following the noise, as silent as a panther.

Then, from the top of the steps, he beheld a scene so strange that he couldn't quite believe it for days afterwards. In the middle of a large open space, surrounded by piles of money and a mountain of custard creems, sat a group of people in white coats. They were passing round a canister with a tube attached to it. One end of the tube was stuck in the top of the canister and other was used to inhale the gas. Each person put this end of the tube in their mouth and breathed in. The person who had just done this now spoke and his voice was high pitched and squeaky. The others fell about laughing and because they had also breathed in the gas, they, too, sounded like giggling mice.

Why were they doing this? Your guess is as good as mine.

There were other goodies, clearly intended for distribution on the streets, watched over by men with dual cartridge pistols (rubber and paper pellets) and ferocious basset hounds.

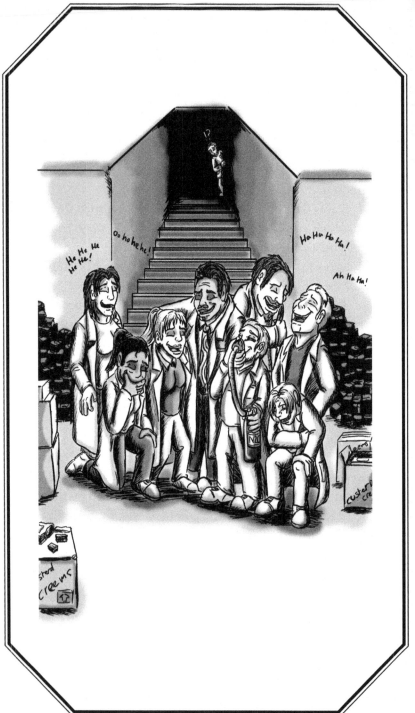

As delicately as any ballet dancer, Agent Pindy retraced his steps and waited until he was clear of the building, before alerting those who had gathered. Within seconds the warehouse was overrun with agents and pretenders alike, the guards overpowered with superior weaponry (class A issue water pistols) and the villains rounded up. However two gang members crept away into the dark unobserved, their pockets stuffed with money.

A radiophonic device crackled into life and one of the villains shouted into it before he could be stopped. 'Don't come back here. We've been rumbled. Go to point K. Repeat. Go to point K.'

Agent Pindy grabbed the device to check it for a tracker. Modern devices had trackers which could pinpoint where it had last been used. Luck was not on his side, and trying to ask any of this lot was worse than useless. They sounded like giggling mice on fast forward!

Then he heard the sound of a car engine starting up and dashed outside to stop the escaping gang members. It was too late. The car was thrusting forward, eager to be gone. Agent Pindy had to make do with a couple of letters from the number plate and the car make, model and colour, which he duly radioed in.

Back in the warehouse no one talked. They giggled, laughed, howled like hyenas, but no one talked. Each suspect was taken off for questioning and Gloria Incisor found herself in a room with Captain Colin. She drew in her breath at the sight of him, his teeth glinting and his eyes glittering. Slowly he began to whirl round to a timeless rhythm in his head, known to dragon slayers the galaxy over. On and on he went, using his famous dragon slayer routine, dancing round the suspect, parrying with an imaginary sword, until she became tired of watching him and buckled under the pressure.

The shame of it all was obvious. She was from a noble family of dentists, proud to offer their services to the poor, free of charge. But then her father had become greedy; had seen how money was to be made by ensuring a never ending supply of patients and raising charges.

At first she had resisted, but then had found a taste for the life style and had been recruited, along with the other members of her family, into the cartel. They had formed the Laughing Gas Gang.

The MO was so clear – where else would a plentiful supply of such gas be obtained? The shopkeepers had been held in thrall, threatened with fillings they didn't need, unless they kept quiet.

'I have one last question for you,' said Captain Colin, threatening to whirl and make Gloria's head spin again. 'Where is point K?'

'I don't know,' admitted the dizzy dentist. 'Some of us knew about some of the gang's locations but no one knew about all of them. It seemed safer that way.'

Gloria was led away to the cells, having taken off her badge herself.

'I don't deserve to be called a dentist,' she whispered in her shame.

Captain Colin sat with his stockinged feet on his desk, enjoying a well earned break. He had cracked the case with his excellent team, but still had no idea about where the rest of the gang hid out. Where was point K?

His mobile telephonic device sounded and the earpiece told him that a car matching the description of the getaway vehicle used earlier in the day had been seen, heading into the labyrinth – a dark and dangerous part of the City to the south.

Putting his shoes on his feet in an instant, the Captain scrambled a helicopter. Within minutes he was circling over the labyrinth, searching it with infrared cameras, until a car was spotted.

The spotlight swung round and highlighted the vehicle. It was the car alright and the occupants were ready for flight. Not two streets away a Justiciary car was nosing its way forward.

So began an intricate game of chess, played out on an earthly board by a sky bound player. Captain Colin had to anticipate the moves of the driver and plot his own accordingly. The driver of the getaway car, panicked by the presence of the helicopter, began making all sorts of errors, using diversionary tactics which would be great for dodging another car but which were worse than useless for shaking off a helicopter.

In a move of sheer incompetence the gang drove up a dead end and Captain Colin moved his chess piece (the pursuit car) into a fishtail manoeuvre. Checkmate! The gang members had nowhere to run and were arrested on the spot.

The accolades for Captain Colin, Agent Pindy and the rest of the team were many and various. Being generous and a true leader, he shared every moment of the glory and the credit.

Sentencing for the cartel was swift. It consisted of community dentistry for life for the dentists involved, as well as returning all the money and goods to the victims; and for the touts, five year sentences working in three city charities.

It hit Captain Colin that taking to the air had been the key to finishing the Laughing Gas Gang. Flying had enabled him to attain his goal, to have a world view, where other means would have failed.

And the sheer beauty of looking down on the world like a map, of seeing it in all its glory (even the labyrinth) struck him. The sense of freedom, of invincibility was liberating. A man who flew was a man who took risks and revelled in doing so; was a man in the process of setting himself free.

The second piece of his heart glided smoothly into place.

At point K a lone figure was speaking into a telephonic device. 'Is that the Piper? This is Milk Tooth. I am coming to the mines.'

TRAVAIL THREE: BEA AND THE BULLY

Whenever he came to visit Captain Colin, Mayor Chillblain liked to pace up and down. He did this when preparing for his speeches and he found that it gave him space to think. But for those watching him, it might make them seasick! Up and down, down and up...oh dear.

Our intrepid Captain was at his desk this winter morning, waiting for the Mayor to share his thoughts. Mayor Chillblain paused, turned, squared his shoulders and spoke.

'We have low crime and the City is certainly safe, but do we have enough projects and places to keep our young people interested, Captain?'

Captain Colin opened his mouth to reply, but Mayor Chillblain ignored him. He was on a roll. 'Just yesterday, my own son was complaining about having nothing to do. Then, as I was going to the office, I saw youngsters lolling on a wall near the sports centre. Lolling; in winter! Well, once they start lolling, it's a slippery slope.'

Captain Colin was just about to respond when a call on his mobile telephonic device interrupted the flow of his thoughts. He took it out of its holster, with an apologetic look at the Mayor.

'Captain Colin at your service,' he answered.

It was his wife, Mary. 'CC (that was her own personal nickname for her husband), you need to come home, quickly. It's Beatrice.'

Since calls like these were as rare as vegetarian dragons or carnivorous squirrels, Captain Colin knew this was serious. 'I am on my way,' he said, snapping his device shut.

'Mayor, I am sorry but that was my wife and I need to go home. Can we carry on this very important discussion at a later date?'

The Mayor was left nodding at a space where Captain Colin had been, as he was now exiting the building at top speed, leaving a trail of sparks on the Justiciary lino.

It was clear that Mary was agitated, her kind face in a frown. Captain Colin kissed her cheek and raised his eyebrows in a question. Mary placed her finger on her lips and pointed to the living room door. Captain Colin could just see the edge of the sofa and a blond plait hanging from it. It looked lonely and sorry for itself, that single plait, even though it had a twin and was attached to Beatrice's head.

Beatrice was in tears, her glasses a bit steamed up, and her face a little red. Captain Colin put his hand on Mary's shoulder to move them both out of earshot and asked softly, 'So what happened?'

'Bea was on her way to school about three weeks ago, when she bumped into Millicent Partridge, the resident school tough nut, on their way through the school gates. It was an accident, but Millicent hassled Bea in the break and extorted her dinner money from her. It's happened every day since.' Mary spoke in a low voice.

'I didn't know until today. She is very upset, but when I suggested contacting the school, she became almost hysterical, saying that it would only make things worse. I didn't know what else to do, so I called you.'

She paused. 'Darling, I am going to ask you to handle this as Bea's Dad, not as the resident city hero.'

Captain Colin gave his wife a big hug. He knew how she devoted herself to her family and how great she was. This was a real crisis.

'I understand, but we can't promise Bea that we won't speak to the school, because bullying of any sort is against city school policy.' He paused, his eyebrows meeting in a frown.

This was not a small or medium sized dragon – this was the biggest kind of dragon there was; a beast that stopped people being treated in the way they should be, because of one person's ego.

'So,' said Mary softly. 'What do we do? How do we protect Bea and stop this Partridge child from doing the same thing again?'

Some minutes later, having agreed together what to do, Beatrice's parents came into the sitting room to speak to her.

'Daddy,' she cried and hugged Captain Colin tightly, her arms around his neck. He hugged her back and then sat with her on the sofa, her hand in his.

'Darling, Mum has told me what happened. Is there anything you want to tell me, too?'

Bea shook her head. 'I told Mum everything. It was an accident but Millie pretended that I did it on purpose and now I know she's going to be there, waiting for me. Dad, I don't want to go back there. Mum could teach me here, couldn't she?' There was such sadness in her voice that it almost completely destabilised her parents' agreed approach, but they resisted.

They told her that they loved her and didn't want to upset her, but that this was not right. If Millicent got away with doing things like this once, what was to stop her from doing it again? Beatrice needed to go back to school and her parents would speak to the Head Teacher, Ms Perrytweet.

Beatrice shouted and pleaded, but her parents did not change their minds. So she said in a low voice, 'I hate you,' and went out to the tree house – her thinking place. Captain Colin and Mary sat on the sofa looking at one another. 'Well, CC, that went well.'

'I have to get back,' Captain Colin said, 'but I will be home before the twins.' He kissed Mary and she nodded.

Back at the Justiciary, Mayor Chillblain was still seated in Captain Colin's office and, when the latter arrived, leapt up.

'Is everything alright?' His voice showed real concern. He admired Captain Colin and was also a father.

Captain Colin shook his head and explained briefly what had happened. 'The thing is that I have to wear two hats. On the one hand I want to protect Bea, but on the other hand I have to look at the wider picture. Mayor Chillblain, we have to make the anti-bullying policy work.'

The two men were closeted for quite some time.

When Alison and Christopher got home and saw Dad's car in the driveway, they knew something was up. Rushing inside they quickly learned what had happened. At twelve they were a couple of years older than baby Bea, as they called her. Neither had any idea about what had been going on, as they were now at the big school across the road.

'Bullying? That's awful,' said Alison.

'Bea in trouble? Whoever it is had better watch out!' threatened Christopher.

They immediately went out to the tree house to find their sister and, sure enough, she was there, knees hunched up to her chin and a scowl on her face to alarm the bravest knight! She had been there all day despite the cold, refusing food and drink. Mary could only watch through the window as a twin sat on either side of Beatrice and put an arm around her shoulders.

They were out there a long time.

Captain Colin and Mary will never know what they talked about in that tree house, because even the wisest parents know that children have secrets from them. But when they came back in, Beatrice was smiling again and agreed to her parents coming to the school the following morning.

The Head Teacher, Ms Demelza Perrytweet, was a woman, whose thin body had been stretched over an elongated frame, making her very angular. She was strict but adored the children and was very well respected.

She showed Captain Colin, Mary and Beatrice into her office. She listened first to Beatrice, then to the parents, nodding wisely like a bobbing owl.

'Well,' she said, when the story had been told and the remedy proposed. 'We need to gather the staff and children together and I know just the thing.'

Occasionally there was an emergency or extraordinary assembly called. The last one had been to congratulate two students on winning places to the Federation of Homeland Cities (FHC) top two universities, Camford and Oxbridge.

This one came as a complete surprise, as teachers received their instructions to bring their children to the hall straight after the morning break, instead of going back to classes. The staff were briefed by Mary and Captain Colin. The children all filed into the hall, and the teachers sat across the stage. The sight of Captain Colin, in his finest uniform, caused many hearts to flutter and many mouths to mutter. What was happening? Why was *he* here?

Ms Perrytweet stood up, her face stern behind her glasses. 'I have called you all here today because it has been brought to my attention that one or two of you have behaved in a manner to bring shame on this establishment.'

Gasps went round the hall and Millicent Partridge smirked.

Ms Perrytweet continued. 'I can promise you that bullying will not go unpunished and I am giving those persons the chance to make themselves known to me now.'

Silence followed – the longest silence you can imagine. No one moved. Millicent Partridge played with her hair and looked glaringly at her friends, who looked scared. She turned round and caught Beatrice's eye. Her look said, 'watch out.'

Beatrice wanted to run out of the room, but stayed where she was, holding the sides of her seat with her hands, her heart thundering and her eyes blinking at about the same rate. Then she saw her parents there and felt calmer.

'Very well,' said Ms Perrytweet at last. 'You leave me no choice. All school trips and privileges are revoked for the rest of this term. I know you will think that this is very unfair, but I am left with no choice. School dismissed. Please go back to your classes quietly and with no fuss.'

Well, there were tears and tantrums, as some children were due to go on an art trip and others on a skiing trip. Cancellation meant chaos and the next twenty four hours crawled by. Angry parents called in, demanding to know what was happening and asking why their children were so upset. What was the matter with the school? Why didn't it have an effective way to deal with such matters?

It was a very quiet night in Captain Colin's household. Bea hardly said a word, but seemed to eat well enough and then played 'Mystery History'™ with her brother and sister. 'Mystery History'™ was a hilarious game, in which contestants picked up clues to match the famous historical character to the deed they had done. The first person to do so won the round. Bea loved history and was now three rounds ahead of her nearest rival.

There was determination and disgruntlement on children's faces in equal measure the following day. Despite winning her game and assuring everyone she was fine, Beatrice had cried herself to sleep, thinking that she was to blame. Only Millicent, thinking herself invincible, sauntered into school the next day like she had no cares at all. She had met up with the gang yesterday afternoon, buying their loyalty with sweets and threatening them with exclusion from the gang if they ratted on her.

Oh dear, Millicent. How often is it said that pride comes before a fall? And fall she did, as one by one the members of her gang crept in to see Ms Perrytweet, fearing the wrath of their schoolmates far more than Millicent's anger.

She was sitting on the benches at break time when it happened.

This was an area in the playground for all children but Millicent and her gang had taken it over and sitting there was only allowed with her express permission. Ms Perrytweet came outside, spoke to the teacher on duty and then made her way across to the benches.

'Millicent Partridge, I would like a word with you.'

Millicent almost lost her cool. She looked around at her gang for support only to realise that they had all slunk off and were watching from the edge of the playground.

Not to lose face, she stood up, shrugged and said, 'Whatever.'

'My office, now,' said Ms Perrytweet in that quiet voice that meant business and Millicent felt her cool ebbing.

It was just after half past ten when Captain Colin's mobile telephonic device burst into song again. He answered it. It was Mary and, no sooner had the call ended, than he was on his way to school.

Millicent had been named and would be dealt with separately. But Ms Perrytweet wanted Captain Colin to address the school about this matter. A second assembly had been called and the children filed in, looking sullen and upset. The atmosphere that morning had been horrible. They saw Captain Colin and this made them even crosser. Next they would be having their break times cancelled!

Captain Colin, who was on stage with the teaching staff, rose to his feet. He stood taller than any pygmy and shorter than any giant, his eyes flashing and his cheeks rubicund. He surveyed the sea of cross children and smiled.

'My name is Captain Colin,' he began, 'and some of you will know me as the Head of the Justiciary. My job is as much about keeping truth and fairness alive, as it is about delivering villains, slaying dragons and righting wrongs.

'But I am also a parent and I was also at school, a long, long time ago.' Several children smiled, despite themselves.

'We become who we are as adults through our experiences at school, influenced by the people we meet, the friends we make and the challenges that we face. And we have choices about how we behave and what we value.'

The children were listening now, realising that he was talking to <u>them</u> and taking <u>them</u> seriously.

'Bullying is a terrible thing. It is not about valuing another person. It is about thinking you are better than them. And that feeling comes from a place inside yourself, which tells you that you are not really good enough. No one here needs to bully anyone else. All of you have the right to be here. The school, your friends, your parents, even the Justiciary,' said with a smile, 'can show you the way, but the choices can be yours. So I need your help because you can make a difference in your school, together.

'Let this be the last time that I have to stand here and talk about bullying. Let the next time I come here be for a reason that makes me proud of this school. Thank you.'

He sat down midst clapping and cheering and then the children filed out. After a quick word with Ms Perrytweet in her office and a kiss for Mary and Beatrice, he zoomed back to work at a sensible zoom speed and tackled the papers that piled up on his desk, until the sun set.

Then in the gloom of the wintry evening, his telecomputer burst into life. It was an a-mail (mail that travelled the airwaves and, through the miracle of modern technology, entered the telecomputer through a vent and transposed into text).

It was from Beatrice. She wrote:

Come home, Dad, we miss you.

The next day was Saturday and Captain Colin's children were studying and shopping in equal measure. And Captain Colin?

He studied the newspaper, unaware that part three of his heart had just crept in and snuggled down next to parts one and two.

And what of Millicent and her family, I hear you ask. Did they learn from this and seek to change her behaviour for the better? Sadly not all lessons stick.

Her parents, who really thought they were rather better than everyone else, moved Millicent to a private school, which costs a lot of money. They sat in their big house feeling smug and, if any of them ever wondered why other people were not as impressed with them as they were with themselves, they never ever admitted it.

TRAVAIL FOUR: THE
DISAPPEARING DRAGON

'It was terrible,' the young girl said, glad of the blanket around her and the hot sweet tea that had been thrust into her hand. 'As big as an aeroplane, but breathing fire. The pilot had to swerve or we would all have ended up...'

She couldn't go on. It was too upsetting and the team of agents who were with the passengers from flight TC123 worked sensitively to get the information, through eye witness accounts. They worked around the clock.

Captain Colin was in his office admiring his new invisible ink fountain pen (the ink was invisible to the naked eye until the document had been grilled lightly on both sides for 57 seconds exactly), when his second in command, Lieutenant Quested, burst in.

'Sir,' she cried, 'we have a real situation on our hands. The airport is in uproar.'

Captain Colin jumped into his car and sped across the City (minding the speed limits) until they reached the airport. Instead of the hubbub of taxiing aircraft and passengers checking in, or being collected, his eyes met a very different scene.

Sitting in rows, arms crossed, airport staff had placed themselves behind a barricade that read simply,

Too dangerous. Please help.

Captain Colin walked forward, the sun glinting on his rubicund cheeks, his face set in a thoughtful expression. He approached the first person, who happened to be Vice Air Traffic Controller (Tuesdays and Thursdays).

'I am an outsider here, but I would like to help. Can you explain why you are all out here and what you are hoping to achieve?'

Mr Spock was his name and he replied as follows.'Captain, for the last seven nights, all aeroplanes landing and taking off have been terrorised by an unknown aircraft. On the super scanner radar screen it looks the size of a big aeroplane, but in the sky it looks… it looks like it has wings and breathes fire.'

He stopped, feeling silly, but Captain Colin was incredibly alert. Could it be…was it possible that…this was the work of a really big dragon?

'I need to know the approximate wingspan and projectile shooting distance of the flame,' he stated. 'Does anyone have a photographic image?'

The young girl (our heroine from earlier), stepped forward and signalled nervously that she did.

'I had my instamatic. If you develop the picture, you might be able to use it.'

'Good thinking,' cried Captain Colin and smiled at her. 'There is a job for you on my team when you are old enough.'

The girl sighed and blushed with pleasure and willingly gave up her instamatic for evidence. In the twinkling of an eye, it was whisked across town to the Justiciary for development.

Back in his office, Captain Colin was waiting for the news, his mobile telephonic device at his ear. Next to him, Lt Quested had her head buried in a copy of 'Swat,' the official guide for the classification of dragons. They were categorised according to wing span, projectile flame length and dive speed, as well as other things. Her boss had not asked his earlier questions at the airport by accident. He knew what he was asking.

The picture was back in an instant, together with a table of mathematical calculations which showed a wingspan of 20 goblins (or metres in modern measurement) and a projectile flame length of ten. A goblin is measured from the tip of his hat to the ends of his toe nails. This was not only a large sized dragon, but came perilously close to being a dragonus maximus.

As Lt Quested rushed away to brief the special team of agents who would assist in this mission, Captain Colin put a 'Do not disturb' sign on his door and, in the privacy of his own office, drew down his dragon slayer's almanack and slowly turned to page 13 – how to dispose of a dragonus maximus without exposing the population of a large city to undue danger or terror.

He read, his kind eyes focused. His breathing was long and steady, his whole body still with the effort of his concentration. Then, finally, he rose and called his team.

'It's a big one,' Lt Quested had told them, 'and that is no joke.'

He faced them. 'There is undeniable evidence of a dragon in our skies, terrorising our citizens and interrupting their holiday plans. This has resulted in an unprecedented strike by the airport staff. Such a thing has never occurred and we, guardians of the City, must make things right again.'

He paused, chest heaving, eyes alight with the flame of duty, before continuing. 'There are things we don't know. Where does this dragon live? Who is its owner?'

'I want you to get out there, put your ears to the ground and come back with what you know. Have they been fully briefed, Lt Quested?'

She nodded. 'Yes, Captain – fully, completely and absolutely so.'

After their departure, he spent many hours practising dragon slaying manoeuvres on the agents' training range. He was the only agent in the whole City anywhere near qualified to handle the weaponry required for such a huge task. He thrust and parried, rotated and swerved, until his heart raced and his whole body was whirling around one small, still centre spot.

When the time came, he would be ready.

It was Lt. Quested who provided the first major breakthrough. She had spent the night at the airport and had seen the events in the night sky for herself. Then, swallowing her fear, all her training coming to the fore, she had cycled on her velociped in the direction the dragon flew off in, tracking it back to... a house in the south sector.

She blinked. A dragon had landed in the garden and, as she peered in through the window, she could only see an elderly man.

She knocked on the door, badge at the ready as proof of who she was. She explained her purpose in being there and the elderly man invited her in.

'You are quite welcome to look but I can assure you that there are no dragons here at present. May I make you a cup of tea while you search?'

And search she did, high and low, but her quest was in vain. Drinking her tea and thanking the gentleman, she took her leave and wheeled her velociped back to the Justiciary, in the central sector.

The following twenty four hours turned up nothing and the same thing happened the following night; only this time there were only two flights that took off, instead of twenty, and travel agencies all over town reported worryingly low bookings for holidays and city visitors.

Captain Colin was with his team, the following morning. 'Team, is there anything, anything at all that you can give me to work with?'

The team wracked their brain and traced back through what they had gleaned as evidence. Suddenly Lt Quested sprang up out of her chair and frightened a small mouse, which had come to see what all the fuss was about.

'The man, the man, the man,' she stammered. 'He said, "there are no dragons here at present". So what if there was a dragon there, but it was out when I called?'

Some of the agents began to laugh. 'Oh yes – it saw you coming so it popped round the corner and hid – a dragonus maximus peering at you from over the garden fence.'

Captain Colin held up his hand. 'Team, we do not laugh at one another, but with one another. We have to work together. I need to check something and I will be back directly.' His voice was stern. 'This is a citywide emergency.'

His mind racing almost as fast as his feet (he was wearing his favourite red stockings), he ran back to his office and looked in his dragon slayer's almanack. Something had jogged a memory. Dragons weren't always dragons, as you would think. Sometimes they were…ah, yes, this was the page.

He read…***there are spells that can help a human take on dragon form***. So, what if the dragon had not been a real dragon but a human spell binder in dragonish form? He raced back to the room where his team sat, the nylon on his feet almost creating sparks on the lino.

As he entered the room, Lt Quested jumped up and toppled her chair. This time the mouse retreated, affronted at all the noise.

'Sir – what if the man I spoke to was a spell…?'

'Binder,' finished the Captain triumphantly. 'Well done, Lt Quested, you have also been thinking laterally. The dragon was nowhere to be seen when you got to the house because…'

It was like a game of tennis and the others were getting dizzy, their heads turning first one way then the other.

'…it assumed another shape ***before*** I got there.' Lt. Quested finished triumphantly.

There was a deathly calm in the room. Now they would have to figure out how to deal with a dragonus maximus. Captain Colin spoke slowly.

'As you know, I am a qualified dragon slayer (small and medium sized dragons), but I am not qualified to slay a dragonus maximus. I have been practising, but it is not enough. We will need to place the house under covert observation to understand when the human spell binder changes.

'One thing I do know,' he added, 'is that things like daylight can affect the spell's ability to bind.'

It was done. Under a cloud smudged sky, the sun just tipping off the horizon, two agents lay watching the house. Their patience was soon rewarded.

An elderly man went out into the garden and on into the meadow beyond, through a wooden gate in a tall fence. He walked and, as he walked, seemed to be muttering some kind of incantation under his breath.

Before the agents' very eyes, his skin turned into scales, his arms into wings, his nails into claws and his mouth into snapping jaws. It was frightening but the agents remembered everything they had been taught in bravery training and stayed where they were. They watched as the man morphed totally into a dragon and flew off against the darkening sky in the direction of the airport.

As soon as the coast was clear they entered the house noiselessly, through the back garden. Donning gloves, they began to search (legally under the Incantation Law, section 37, points i to iii, which states that a spell cannot be used for nefarious purposes and, if it is, then any method can be legally used to stop it). There were piles of books and mountains of tea cups – clearly being a dragon was thirsty work.

Just when it seemed hopeless, Agent Bubble turned to Agent Squeak and motioned her to come across. 'Look', he whispered.

Agent Squeak's eyes widened. She saw a very old book, bound with cracked and stained leather, open at a page with a picture of a dragon so terrifying that it would scare the hair off a lion. Underneath the illustration, in copperplate lettering, they read the following (but did not repeat it aloud, as they had learned in spell training).

THIS MY TREASURE TAKE
AND ME A DRAGON MAKE

Grabbing the book and knocking a tea cup flying, Agents Bubble and Squeak made their way back to the Justiciary. From there they sent a message to the team at the airport, via their mobile telephonic devices, alerting them to the progress that had been made.

Next they took the book to Code Decryption Command, a crack team of experts who decoded anything from secret messages to spells. They were ready and ran the spell through Indecipherable - their trusty code breaking machine.

Indecipherable wheezed and spluttered, coughed and cranked, but, within a couple of minutes, had shot a ribbon of paper out of its side. This paper was filmed and had to be pinned up against a backlit screen to be read.

It read:

Spell origin: Orthodox Druid, circa 1677 (May)
Spell purpose: to enable human spell binder to take on dragon form (or other)

Antidote: to be whispered in the ear of the dragon
as it is flying

Thy borrowed shape forsake
Thee as thou were I make

Well, that was clear enough, but who would be able to fly close enough to the dragon? With time on the run, the two agents thanked their colleagues and hastened to where Dragon Command had been set up.

They gave the paper to Captain Colin and waited with bated breath as he scanned the contents. Then he looked up, his kind face serious, his cheeks pale.

'Scramble the Pied Piper Arrow,' he commanded. There was an audible intake of breath.

With its Lycoming IO-360--C1C6 engine and Sabre Tip Blade propellers, its Vespucci Skynav and Hamelin Autocontrol, it was the pride of the Justiciary aero fleet.

In a now cloudless sky the colour of indigo, the dragon was running amok. The delight of swooping into the path of oncoming aircraft, seeing the flames from its nostrils reflected in the whites of the eyes of the terrified pilots, was addictive.

Down below there was chaos. People ran screaming as flame bolts hit the runways and sent fountains of sparks up into the blackness. The air traffic control tower was empty and aeroplanes were coming in without radio contact. It had disaster written all over it.

Suddenly a small, stirring noise broke through the din. The steady whirr of sabre tipped propellers sent the air helter skelter either side of them. At the heart of the darkness sat Captain Colin, his megaphonic device by his side.

His face reflected in the glass of the cockpit looked almost demonic, illuminated from underneath by the greenish light of the console. He looked straight ahead, the dragon in his sights.

He flew straight at the dragon, causing it to swerve out of surprise, rather than fear. What ensued was an aerobatic dance; dragon and aeroplane rising and falling, spinning and looping, turning and twisting.

Darts of flame shot from the dragon's nostrils, sometimes gilding the wing tips with a bronze glow. Finally, flying up above the dragon, Captain Colin set his plane on autocontrol and switched on his megaphonic device. Straddling the cockpit, he slid the glass back and the skin on his face rippled with the gravitational pull.

Should the dragon deviate from his current course by one length of a goblin's toenail, then all would be lost. But the dragon's curiosity got the better of him and he waited, as the Pied Piper Arrow whistled past. Some words were shouted and, below, necks craned and mouths open in amazement, the whole of the City stood silent in watchful prayer.

The words danced across the air currents towards the dragon, forming a phrase, knitting into a sentence, and then a verse. The foolish creature strained its ears, wanting to make sense of what the Captain had said, the better to taunt him later.

Then the very worst thing that can happen to a dragon in mid flight happened. Snapping jaws became a mouth, claws nails, scales skin and wings arms. There,

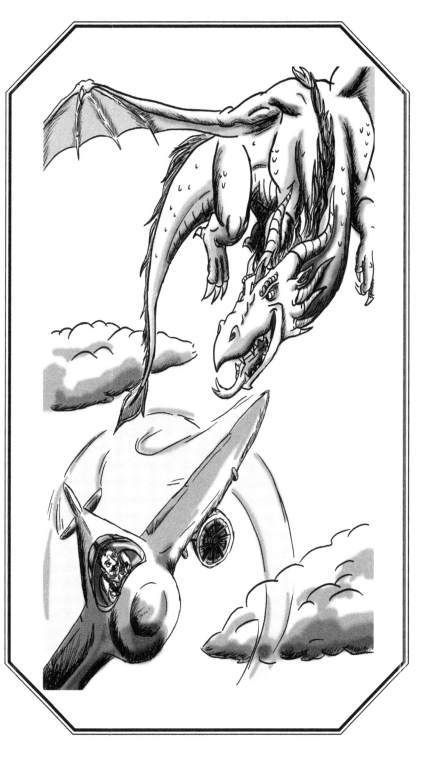

suspended in the night sky for an everlasting moment, was a man; just a man.

The world gasped as he plummeted, faster than a swooping eagle, towards the ground below. Then the world double gasped as Captain Colin went into a tailspin and, in a manoeuvre worthy of an entry in the Guinness Book of Records, flattened out, flew up under the man and scooped him into the cockpit.

Back on terra firma, the man was led away, winded, bruised and contrite. The City once again blessed their luck at having Captain Colin to right wrongs and slay dragons (though some churls would claim that that was not a slaying as that was not a dragon).

The story that emerged later was a very sad one indeed. The man, a former professor at the City University, lived alone in a house under the flight path in and out of the City, doing a postal doctorate in the arcane arts. His fascination with spells and their powers had reached fever pitch at about the same time as his frustration with the constant noise of air traffic overhead and you can understand, reader, what happened next.

But a plan to teach the City a lesson and put pay to the noise went awry and was replaced by the corrupting force of power, when it is misused. Justice was done and the perpetrator was sentenced to a life sentence of writing dictionary entries at the City Library.

Captain Colin, Lt Quested and their team were the heroes of the hour. They had risked life and limb, pitted their wits against one of Nature's oldest and most powerful creatures and had saved the City.

Later, in the quiet of his shed, parts of an engine in his hand, Captain Colin reflected that he had gone, on that day, to the heart of the darkness and shone the light of truth on it and now the shadow was gone. Somehow, a chink of light had also appeared, illuminating some of the darkness that still lay at the heart of his heart, now four parts complete.

And in the spell binder's house, where the tea cup had fallen, the leaves had spilled out and formed a heart.

Travail Five: Treedom

Out beyond the edge of the north sector of the City stood a shady copse, full of old oak, ash and rowan trees, their branches laden with moss, their trunks striped and pitted with plant and animal activity. The trees didn't appear to do much except move their branches with a passing wind and shed their leaves at the right time. But for those of you who think that this is all that trees get up to, think again.

What you thought was the sighing of the wind in the branches is in fact the whispering of one tree to another, telling tales, asking questions and conversing with Nature. The copse was a real community, teeming with birds and insects and small creatures. In short, it was, despite its sleepy appearance, a thriving colony.

It was into this peaceful oasis that a very agitated pigeon flew; crash landing on a branch and making itself dizzy. It did a break dancing spin, flapped its wings as though it were throwing some shapes on the dance floor and righted itself to avoid bouncing on its head in the dirt below.

'I'm all a to do,' it announced and no one really took any notice. This particular pigeon had a reputation for drama and being all a to do was its way of life.

Affronted at the lack of response, it settled in front of an owl and cooed. The owl opened one eye, sighed and sat up.

'What it is, Pigeon?'

'Owl, I have heard something dreadful.' And it all came tumbling out, a jumble of words and cooing, which when put together made a terrible message.

'I was rooting in the city centre for some tasty snacks and there were several suits sitting on a bench, having lunch. I usually listen in on people, to see what they are talking about. Coo coo.

'Anyway, Owl, they were talking about plans to extend the City and I was just about to bob away when I heard them mention our area, so I stayed on like a true spy, to glean more.'

Owl repressed a sigh. Pigeon was convinced that it descended from a line of noble spy pigeons involved in all sorts of espionage. Pigeon cooed and went on.

'They plan to cut the copse down,' lowering its voice, 'to make way for housing. I was so shocked that I flew straight here.'

Trees have acute hearing and this news travelled very quickly along branches and root systems. What humans take for rustling leaves was like drums, beating out a message. Soon all the trees and wildlife had heard and, that night, for the first time since one of the oldest oaks has been an acorn, a council was called.

They debated far into the night. This news was terrible and they must do something, but what?

'I think we should stay put and fight,' said one rowan tree, nervously shaking its boughs. 'We were here first and we have to live somewhere.'

'Have you ever faced down a digger?' asked an ash tree crossly. 'I have and let me tell you, it's not nice. In the end, we moved.'

'We have to make a stand,' stated the council leader, an oak so ancient that no one knew how old it really was. 'We have to march to the City, take root in the Council Square and tell them what we think of their plan.'

'Ridiculous,' chorused a group of saplings more interested in hanging out than standing up for their civil rights. 'Too much like hard work.'

'If you want to be cut in two, you are going the right way about it,' snapped a pine tree, replanted here by mistake instead of on forestry commission land three miles up the road. 'And I know what I am talking about. We pines are genetically bred to be culled.' It shivered. 'No thanks.'

Gradually all the dissenting voices buckled under one grand and tricky plan. They would march by night until they reached the City. If you think that trees don't march, check out the trees in your garden on different days. Can you be sure they are exactly where they were when you left them?

The planning went on further into the night.

Captain Colin was briefing his team on the events for the forthcoming day when a call came into the Justiciary.

It was a very bewildered builder, called Mr Render. 'I think there have been vandals on the proposed building site in the north sector.'

'Vandals?' asked the call handler. 'What has gone missing?'

'Um...the trees,' said Mr Render, aware of how ridiculous that sounded.

'The trees,' repeated the call handler, rolling his eyes. There was a crank call every minute.

'Yes, the trees,' repeated Mr Render, sensing waves of disbelief down the phone line. 'Come and see for yourselves.'

Agents were dispatched immediately and an extraordinary sight met their eyes. Imagine a dug up field, with earth and small mountains of soil everywhere. All the trees had been uprooted and had gone. The agents shook their heads. In the background they could hear Mr Render talking.

'I've told the cops about the copse but they're none the wiser.'

The trees and their companions moved slowly under cover of night, while their bird friends pinpointed locations for rest during daylight. Their first resting place had been on the edge of another wood - perfect camouflage.

Now the pigeon had spotted a field, empty and unremarkable, at the back of a farm. Here the trees, young and old, settled, digging their roots into the cool, damp earth and grunting their satisfaction, glad to rest. Having blisters in your roots is no laughing matter.

Farmer Holly was a farmer right through to his bones. Every morning since he could remember, he had got up at five o clock, made a cup of tea and drawn back the curtains to look out over his land. And so he did this morning – except that where there should have been a field there was a wood!

He stood for a split second in complete surprise, mouth open, and tongue out, eyes popping out of his head. Then, dropping his cup in the sink, he ran out of the kitchen into the garden in his socks. This was no illusion – those trees were real. He ran back in and called the Justiciary.

The following day Captain Colin, his rubicund cheeks drawn in, was concentrating. A missing copse and an unexpected new wood, both in thirty six hours. It was clear that the two were linked but how? He shook his head. His mobile telephonic device rang and the earpiece spoke to him.

'Captain, you had better come down to the city council offices.'

The usually calm voice of the Lt. Quested sounded so incredibly incredulous, that Captain Colin went straightaway.

As news of his impending arrival spread a ripple of reassurance ran through the crown. The Captain is coming, people said, he'll know what to do.

An unprecedented sight greeted him. In the square in front of the council offices, with its marble fountain and sparkling water, there was…well…there was now a wood. A few dozen trees and assorted wildlife had, quite literally, taken root. It was a beautiful, if unexpected view.

The city Mayor was beetroot with anger in his office, his nose shinier than his mayoral chain. As Captain Colin entered the room he started shouting, 'They cannot stay here. I will have them charged with loitering…and damage to public property…and…'

He fulminated on, while Captain Colin thought for a moment. This was not a dragon slayer challenge and he would require a different approach. Then, turning his back on the red faced Mayor, he went out without a word. It certainly shut the Mayor up, who stood open mouthed, his ranting interrupted.

Whipping off his shoes (some of the crowd swooned at the sight of his stockings) Captain Colin clambered into the low branches of the nearest oak, while the crowd watched agog. The Mayor came to the window.

'I knew it,' he thought. 'That man is having some kind of midlife crisis and will have to go.'

Captain Colin smoothed the bark of the branch on which he was sitting. It felt warm to the touch. He didn't speak Tree (though he was pretty fluent in Dragonish), and tried French as a starter.

'Vous êtes loin de chez vous,' he offered as an opener and was met with silence.

'You are a long way from home,' he tried again, translating into English. 'I want to help you, but you have to help me.'

A rumble started, like light drumming, getting louder and stronger, until it formed slow, comprehensible words. 'We are here to protect our land.'

Captain Colin nodded and his kind eyes were serious. 'You have come from beyond the edge of the City. Is that right? This is a long and unusual journey for trees, which are habitually rooted beings, to make.'

The oak shook its branches, not so dangerously that Captain Colin would fall, but enough to warn that what it was about to say was serious.

'I was small once; a tiny acorn, which fell in some sticky mud and took root. I have been there for over two hundred years, longer than you humans can comprehend. I've been climbed, hugged, photographed and kicked, but always in the same location - from sapling to mighty tree.'

The other trees turned to one another. 'Two hundred years,' they gasped. 'Respect!'

'Now our home is being taken away from us. We have never harmed you. We have provided shelter and shade for you; we keep lovers' initials carved in our bark; we have witnessed teddy bears' picnics and thrown lost balls back to crying children. We have turned carbon dioxide into oxygen to sustain the planet and lots more besides.' This oak knew its stuff.

'Why do you seek to hurt us, when all that we have ever done is care for you?'

Quite a crowd had gathered, as much to see the famous Captain shinning up a tree as to see the trees themselves. It was not every day that a dragon slayer in his stockinged feet chose to sit on a branch and pretend to speak Tree.

'Is it a trunk call?' shouted one merry onlooker, fancying himself as a stand up comedian.

'I'll be-leaf it when it happens,' cried another as laughter went round the crowd.

'If he's talking to trees now, he'll be hugging them next – you just wait and see,' a third person called out.

For what was perfectly comprehensible speech to Captain Colin, up in the branches, was nothing more than the soughing of wind through leaves for the onlookers on the ground. In this era of mobile telephonic devices, a-mail and air travel, the eerie sight of trees in the city centre had been quickly accepted and was a wonder no longer.

'I am asking you to trust me and not to move until I am able to come back to you,' said Captain Colin, as he scrambled down the trunk of the oak. 'I will not be long.'

Once back on terra firma, he put on his shoes much to the disappointment of some in the crowd, straightened up to his shoulder to shoulder with any man height and made for the Mayor's office.

The Mayor was still beside himself and his wife, her chain only slightly smaller, had an equally shiny nose.

'Captain Colin, what is the meaning of this outrage? How dare those trees drag dirt into our clean streets and litter the fountain with their falling leaves! I must insist that you get them removed as quickly as possible. The Bentley was only polished yesterday.' Mrs Chillblain was not a nature lover.

Captain Colin held up his hand. 'Mrs Chillblain, I must ask you to be patient. I need to speak with you and your husband about the plight of these trees.'

Mr Chillblain, the Mayor some five years, drew himself up to his not quite shoulder to shoulder with any other man height and, stepping out onto the speech balcony, equipped with microphones, looked Captain Colin in the chin.

'Now look here, Captain. You are here to serve the City and I am, by virtue of my position, the most important client you have.' Everyone could hear him plainly.

He was about to launch into a speech, but, as the good citizens of the City knew, that meant a forty five minute monologue, during which people whispered to one another, shifted from one foot to the other, secretly listened to their p-pods or just picked their teeth. The Mayor was a good man, but boring.

Captain Colin held up his hand again. 'Sir Chillblain (flattery would get him everywhere), I am aware that this is an unusual event. It is not every day that we have trees marching in protest to our city centre. So we must ask ourselves why this has happened.'

The crowd were listening now, heads turning from the Captain to the Mayor as though they were watching a ping pong match.

'The City has known good economic fortune and has happy citizens. We have telecomputers and a-mail. We have flight and holidays. We also have Nature; a cool breeze, a green field, a sunset over the sea. Nature gives us serenity and reminds us that we are not all about machines. It asks us to live in harmony with it and with one another.

'Let us ask ourselves if we need to breach the City's boundaries, or if we can find another way to encourage people to live and work in our midst, while observing Nature's own laws.'

Mayor Chillblain rubbed his chin and stared at Captain Colin's teeth (it was all he could see from his height). They were fine teeth and white, but this was not a matter of molars.

'Are you suggesting, Captain, that we look at a building programme within the City?' There was a low rumble of support from the engineers, builders, chartered surveyors, interior designers and architects in the crowd.

The Mayor was not a politician for nothing and the crowd were responding. 'Are you suggesting, Captain, that we improve the City's infrastructure to cope with this new development and the people it will need to serve? A roller coaster monorail? New shopping malls? Buses?' There was now a rumble of support from bus drivers, taxi drivers, shoppers and leisure centre owners.

And so it went on. As Mayor Chillblain sensed he was on a roll, he whipped the crowd up into frenzy and later polls would show that his popularity had peaked at an all time high.

The trees had stood patiently all the while, bowing their branches gracefully and limiting all rustling, to catch the conversation and understand the Mayor's words. As the promise of rescue became clearer, a mighty rumbling broke out among the trees. They bent, as though bowing to the men on the balcony and suddenly the crowds felt themselves being swept up into their branches. Even those with a fear of heights felt safe!

'Yeah – respect to the tree massive,' sang the saplings, excited at their first political rally.

'Give it up for the Mayor,' shouted the crowd, 'and the Captain.'

With much cheering, clapping and merriment, the copse made its way back in a stately fashion through the wide streets of the city centre, the narrower residential areas, where the sun shone on neat gardens and rows of washing and finally the paths that led beyond the north sector boundary. People ran to and fro, dropping out of the trees and waving them on their way, promising to visit them soon. It all had the air of a huge outdoor festival.

Calls and a-mails had been flying unseen through the air. Mr Render and his colleagues had been busy and, when the trees beheld their land, it was empty of diggers and other machinery.

The Mayor declared the area an outstanding natural beauty spot and to be forever preserved as it was, while the City was to see some big and welcome changes.

Long after the events of that day, the City remembered its two heroes, Captain Colin and Mayor Chillblain. The saplings grew into trees and talked on many evenings about their march for 'treedom'. The tale became another chronicle and, for Captain Colin, the fifth piece of the jigsaw of his heart.

Travail Six: The Nougat Mines

'I am so tired I can hardly see straight,' grumbled Alison as she sat down to breakfast, one half of her hair in a pigtail and the other in a plait.

Captain Colin and Mary exchanged glances. For days now Alison had seemed exhausted, barely able to drag herself out of bed of a morning. Stumbling over her bags, she walked to school as if in a dream, only to return home that evening, slumbering over supper, unable to recall events of the school day. The other two children were exhibiting the same signs of fatigue. Yet nothing in their normal routine had been disrupted or changed. Nonetheless Alison, Beatrice and Christopher seemed to be sleepwalking through the day and Mary and Captain Colin, like other parents, were becoming concerned.

Alison continued to grumble – unusual in itself – as she poured cereal into her cup by mistake and added water. 'Oh drat,' she exclaimed and, too tired to lift her cup and empty the cereal into her bowl, just hunched over the table and tapped her fingers on it.

There was not even a laugh or a giggle from Beatrice or Christopher, both of whom had dark circles stamped round their eyes. In fact, breakfast had gone from being a noisy, tripping over each other type of activity to one of almost deafening silence.

A letter dropped onto the mat. Mary, who went to retrieve it, was already reading it on the way back to the table. Her sudden loud exclamation of disgust created enough energy for her children to raise their heads.

'Well,' she said, banging the letter down on the table and glaring at her three children in turn. 'I never thought this would happen.'

Four blank faces looked back at her.

All across the City there was consternation breaking out among parents. Family upon family was receiving a similar letter from Ms Perrytweet and other school heads, reporting that children were absent from class without leave. Truancy rates were through the roof.

Moreover, the letters said, the children that were present were worn out. Was there an epidemic of sleeping sickness breaking out? Were children being allowed to stay up late watching unsuitable programmes or playing on their Fandango XM games? No one could say.

On the advice of the school's councillor, Mayor Chillblain called an emergency community meeting in the City Hall that same evening to discuss the matter. Feelings ran high, with parents and teachers berating one another, pointing fingers and shouting while their tired offspring dozed in chairs. It was chaotic and noisy. Eventually Mayor Chillblain managed to restore order.

'Please, citizens, I know you are concerned, but we need to look at the facts of the matter and ask ourselves what we know. There are copies of a league table showing truancy rates for all the schools in the City and you will all agree when you see it that this problem runs right across every school.'

There was no denying the truth of his words – it was there in black and white.

'We need to involve the Justiciary,' cried someone, to universal agreement from those around him. The din got louder and louder and the discussions snowballed until they arrived at Captain Colin's door like an avalanche.

'Captain Colin,' said Mayor Chillblain, drawing himself up to his not quite taller than any pygmy height. 'Your City needs you.'

Some time later, Captain Colin was ruminating – this is a very posh version of thinking. What was happening to these children and how could he and his crack team break the code of this mystery? Captain Colin liked to ask himself questions and it gave him a little glow when he answered them correctly.

All ruminating at an end, he buzzed for two of his most experienced agents to come and see him. As he waited for them, he twirled his moustache, walked several lengths of his office in his stockinged feet and chanted a dragon slayer's good luck rap under his breath.

It went like this...

'Give it up for the dragon
But he's not the only player
So let me hear you give it large
For the City's dragon slayer'

The agents, Cripsy and Crunchy, sat down and faced their boss. He was very honest with them – being the boss did not mean knowing all the answers.

'I'll be honest with you, Crispy and Crunchy. This has really puzzled me and three heads on a problem are better than one.'

'It's not an isolated incident,' started Agent Crispy, 'so I would rule out a school being behind it. All of them are equally affected.'

'I agree,' said Agent Crunchy. 'It doesn't make sense for the parents to be behind this either. No one would want their children at a school that didn't give them the best possible education.'

'We can't rule out magic,' stated Captain Colin in a magnificent voice, twirling his moustache and tapping his toes, which he tended to do when excited.

Two more hours in the meeting and it was clear that this was to be an undercover mission with overt surveillance tactics. (This is much cleverer than covert surveillance as the operatives act so obviously that no one believes that such clumsy twits could actually be spying).

And so it was that a fleet of vans with 'Surveillance'™ painted on the side appeared the very next day, one outside each local school in the City. They were driven by drivers with enormous headphones clamped to their ears and reflecting sunglasses. No one paid them any attention.

In another part of the City a most innocuous man was pulling on some strange garments. A red silk shirt with long billowing sleeves was tucked into knickerbockers of green and red stripes, which in turn were pulled over

silken tights of green. Shoes with curling toes and a striped waistcoat completed his ensemble.

Those who saw him thought a) he was canvassing for the local political party b) he was advertising a restaurant c) he was having a bad shirt day.

As he left his house, he had a brown satchel slung over his shoulder and a tin recorder in his hand. He walked to the edge of the City and, putting the recorder to his lips, began to play a haunting melody that was so delicate and high that it did not pierce the adult ear drum. But the children – they were captivated by the tune and followed it in a trance.

Lines of children moved as though sleepwalking towards those beautiful notes and, behind them, the drivers of the vans revved up their engines and followed them to the edge of the City where they...disappeared. Literally. Gone.

Back at the Justiciary, Captain Colin was sitting with some very confused overt surveillance agents.

'What? Just gone?' asked Captain Colin, his face in a frown.

His bemused colleagues nodded. 'One minute they were there, the next they had vanished. Had we not seen it with our own eyes, we would not have believed it either.'

'We need Witch Warble,' chorused Crispy and Crunchy

Meanwhile, across an invisible line and in a parallel world that curled up next to our world like a cat, the vanished children were toiling under a hot sun. With pickaxes and shovels, they were cutting vast chunks of nougat and putting them into wagons. From the top, the pit looked like a vast, upside down Mr Whippy ice cream, paths tracing its sides, along which the wagons were driven.

If any child stopped or slackened his or her pace just a little, to have a rest under that burning sun, a guard brandishing a toe tickler would appear at their side in the twinkling of an eye. Grabbing their ankle and turning their foot sole up, they would tickle the child until he or she begged for mercy. It's exhausting being tickled by a professionally trained toe tickler and all that laughing and wriggling made them tireder still.

Raw nougat is tough, rough, sticky and hard to extract. Once refined it is still sticky but delicious and smooth. The raw chunks were poured into a giant vat and if you traced the impossibly curling metal pipes to their very end, you could just see the finished bars shooting out of the other end. Each one was caught by a specially trained catcher, wearing a wicket keeper's gloves. They were then piled on pallets and taken to waiting lorries.

Inside an office, a handsome man with beautiful teeth was doing some sums on an electronic abacus and smiling a lot. Yes, it was Milk Tooth from the Laughing Gas Gang, who made his escape earlier in our adventures. He was back in operation and now flooding the streets of the City with a new, chewy, dentition decaying snack. Next to him, the piper was counting a large wad of cash that had just been placed in his hand.

'Lots of lovely lollies, to make lots of lovely lolly,' he sang to himself.

'Pipe down' said Milk Tooth.

Captain Colin was a remarkable man, with a wide network of contacts in the City. A righter of wrongs needs all the backup he can get! And so it was that, on a balmy evening with lots of tired, amnesiac children in their beds, he made his way to the house of one Miss Melody 'Witch' Warble, erstwhile witch and now upright member of the community.

She had got into trouble some years earlier when a white magic trick had gone wrong. The City Zoo was having trouble rearing baby penguins and, as a main attraction, this was a problem. So they had approached Witch Warble to perform a magic trick to help more baby penguins to be born and add to the flock.

Unfortunately two chants had got mixed up. The one for baby penguins and baby giraffes sounded very similar half way through and there had been a shock some weeks later. Baby penguins had been born by the dozen, but with long, graceful necks. The crowds had flooded in to see the 'girguins', as they caught fish with elegant ease and showed a strange fondness for leaves.

The whole thing was referred to the Justiciary and investigated as the zoo had not followed proper protocols by asking a witch to help with an animal programme. As a result, Miss Warble had been stripped of her right to practise any arcane arts for a period of five years.

Now, over a cup of delicious hot ginger beer, Captain Colin explained his predicament. 'It's like a jigsaw, but I don't have the box lid with the picture on it. We know that the children disappear at the start of school and reappear at the end, but they vanish in between.'

Miss Warble thought deeply and tried not to finger the wart on her nose. She was a stout woman with fingers like spatulas and kind eyes.

'Children captivated and disappearing...it's like a fairy story gone bad', she mused. 'Maybe it's an invisible signal for children. It could be a whistle, or music...or a piper!'

'Piper?' Captain Colin was nonplussed.

'Yes. It is a well known fact that pipers play music that only animals and children can hear.' Miss Warble became animated. 'There was a case in another city some years ago, but it was all the cats that disappeared.'

'So someone is luring the children out. But where?'

Miss Warble had been fussing over a dirty glass bowl, which looked as though it had seen better days. She now stared into it, as though the grime and rinse stains could tell her something. Her eyes rolled back and her wart seemed to pop. Just as suddenly, she came to her senses.

'You need to go up high to see the workings of this magic,' she said firmly. 'Wherever the children are going is not visible at ground level. They are in the dream. You have to go above the dream. Yes – that's it. You have to fly above the dream. You have to cut the link between the two worlds. Do that and you will cut the piper's power to lure the children away ever again.'

'Flying!' Captain Colin exclaimed. He rose to his feet. 'Miss Warble, I am in your debt. But tell me, what would you use to cut the link?'

'Bolt cutters,' she responded decisively.

'Miss Warble, you truly are a marvel.' Captain Colin smiled at his friend.

And Miss Warble forgot that she was an aged crone with a warty nose and felt like a debutante at her first ball.

'Thank you,' she smiled as the Captain kissed her fingers.

He was now a man on a mission with no time to lose.

'Scramble the Pied Piper Arrow,' he barked into his mobile telephonic device, making straight for the airfield. 'Meet me there,' he added.

How apt, to catch a piper with a Piper.

The plane was ready when he arrived, the ground crew standing by. Through a great stroke of good fortune, it was also school home time. Captain Colin flew to the city boundary tracing it from south to north. Up he went, taking the aircraft higher and higher, feeling the pressure as he climbed against the blue sky and then, looking down, he saw an amazing sight.

Hordes of children were converging on the City's north sector boundary. As they approached the buildings, they seemed to pass under a live wire of some sort. It was like a piece of trapped lightning, incandescent, throwing sparks, snaking over the air like a blade of electricity, separating the two worlds that the children were moving between.

Emerging into our world, light and warm with the sun, the children rubbed their eyes, stretched their aching limbs, picked up their bags and trailed wearily homewards. Where they came from was visible from the air, but in shadow, like a dark cloud.

Captain Colin knew that severing this link was the only way to stop this child labour and reduce the City's truancy rates. From inside his dragon slayer's kit, behind the plasters and in front of the curly sword, there was a pair of giant, insulated bolt cutters. He drew them out, his other hand on the controls.

Captain Colin was at his most handsome in moments like these. His eyes glowed, his cheeks shone and his teeth were bared in a hero's smile. He manoeuvred the aircraft into a diving position and readied the bolt cutters.

The balance between putting the plane on autopilot, leaning out of the cockpit, cutting the live force field at the right point and stopping the plane from going into a spin was all in a day's work for a righter of wrongs. But this did not make him complacent.

The aircraft hurtled towards the earth like a diver towards water. A bird watcher by the river caught a glint of metal in her binoculars and traced the flight path. She witnessed Captain Colin opening the cockpit, the g force threatening to loosen the elastic in his underpants.

She saw him lean out of the plane at an impossible angle, waving a large pair of secateurs, seeming to cut something and then averting near death by arcing the aircraft back up towards the heavens with only minutes to spare before it landed nose down in the silted riverbed. She gasped and rushed home to tell her family what she had witnessed.

Captain Colin's heart was racing and it felt full to bursting as he landed and made his way back to the Justiciary. Now all they could do was wait.

The next morning the following happened all over the City at the same time.

1. The piper played his recorder, but no sound came out.
2. The nougat mines vanished into thin air, leaving

the dentist sitting in an office on the edge of a lake, feeling very foolish indeed.

3. Children awoke in their beds, feeling refreshed and ready for their breakfast, with no memory of what had happened.

4. Nougat sales and truancy rates in the City went through the floor.

5. There were reports of a man in a funny costume stomping out of the City, muttering to himself and carrying two bits of a broken whistle in his hands.

As for our hero, he returned home to where his family were waiting for him, with their news and their stories. And into the darkness of his heart, a new light fell as piece number six slotted into place.

TRAVAIL SEVEN: THE
SECRET TUNNEL

The whole City was in a state of excitement last experienced only when Mayoress Chillblain had almost split her sides at a Christmas show. She had laughed so hard and so long at the pantomime horse dance that two theatre ushers had to carry her out on a stretcher. Her chortling could be heard from City Hall to the Justiciary.

The City Chronicle trumpeted the amazing engineering feat from its front page with headlines so large that they could be seen at twenty paces.

TUNNEL UNDER THE SEA LINKS US WITH WESTERN COUNTRY.

People shook their heads in amazement and vowed to be the first to take the journey. Imagine going underground and coming out the other side in another country. Bookings literally crammed the airwaves and a-mails flew back and forth. Queues to drive into the tunnel stretched right across the terminal and cameras were snapping everywhere, as amazed travellers marvelled at the sheer size of the tunnel entrance. It was bigger than the wide open mouth of a hungry whale!

Within a few weeks people were speaking of having 'taken the tunnel', as though they had picked it up and carried it with them under their arm. It became the trendy thing to do and, if you hadn't yet done it, you weren't quite part of the 'in' group.

A few meanies tried to make out that the tunnel would be a bad thing, but no one took any notice of them and the excitement continued unabated. It was, those in the know said, almost as wide as a small plane from tip to tip and there wasn't just one tunnel but two; one for going and one for coming back.

Across the shining expanse of sea in Western Country, in a low roofed industrial unit a mile or so inland from the coast, a shadowy figure was rubbing its hands together and laughing demonically to the consternation of those present. It could only be described as shadowy because no one ever saw it. It was just an outline of face with a hooked nose and chin, in profile, projected onto a white wall. When it spoke, its voice was digitally synthesised on a binary system, producing just two pitches. When it laughed, it sounded like a police siren.

'Listen up,' it said to a group of assembled people, crooking its finger to invite them closer. They all crept towards the projected silhouette.

'The digging has finished and the sides of the tunnel are being lined with concrete. In a matter of days we will be able to create a diversion in the tunnel and send a few well chosen visitors on a detour to visit us here.' It laughed and one or two people covered their ears. 'No doubt their concerned relatives will pay good money to get their family members back.'

I expect you remember Florence and Cyril, Captain Colin's parents. They were very proud of their son, as you can imagine and adored their grandchildren. Well, on the morning in question they were terribly excited.

'Have you got the GoCards?' asked Florence for the millionth time, checking her hair in the mirror before placing her best hat on it. A GoCard is like a passport.

'Yes, dear,' replied Cyril, lugging a large orange suitcase towards the front door. 'And food and fuel and money and tickets.'

She turned to him and smiled. He looked just like Captain Colin, but with snow white hair. 'I know that I fuss, my dear, but I am so looking forward to seeing my sister again.'

'I know it's been a long time,' reflected Cyril. 'It must be five years since she moved to Western Country.'

So there you have it. They were off on a trip to Western Country to see Gertrude, Florence's sister. It was like a small adventure; booking the tickets, packing, getting up while the sun was still asleep to catch an early slot. Cyril was a little nervous about driving through such a long tunnel, but, as his son had pointed out, there were no turn offs, so all he had to do was follow his nose until he got to the other end.

They were still chatting as they pulled out of their drive and started off.

'I thought the tickets sales person was so polite,' commented Florence, taking off her hat. 'He took the registration number of the car so meticulously and wished us a pleasant journey.'

Cyril just smiled, marvelling that his wife had put a hat on just to go from the house to the car.

Although fingers of light were only just stretching out over the sky, there was already activity at the Justiciary. An agent was in and seemed hard at work, staring at a computer screen and scrolling down through a long list of numbers in columns. Every few moments she stopped to write one of the numbers on a pad beside her. When this was done, she picked up her mobile telephonic device and called an unknown person.

If someone had looked hard at that device, they might have noticed that it was not standard Justiciary issue. This meant that calls on it could not be traced in the usual way.

Captain Colin was also in and had just finished a call to his parents. 'Have a great time,' he said, 'and give my love to Auntie Gert.' It had been a while since he had seen Auntie Gert, with her exploding hair and love of biscuits.

At the terminal, the cars waited in a long line, like a silver snake. Customs excisers checked GoCards and asked travellers three important questions.

1. Did you pack your bags yourself?
2. What is the purpose of your visit to Western Country?
3. What is the square root of 1679? (you were allowed to use a calculator for this question)

Cyril and Florence gasped as they drove towards the tunnel, under the high arch and into the darkness beyond. In fact, it wasn't dark, but well lit. They could see huge concrete rings lining the tunnel and, in the distance, stopping places built into the side. The road markings were clear and digital signs flashed every so many goblin lengths (or metres if you prefer) telling travellers the distance from their point of origin and to their destination. It was quiet, calm and....easy.

Back in Western Country a small group with a big list had set off down the secret tunnel, which joined the main tunnel about three quarters of the way along. They wore very official uniforms. They saw a car approaching and scanned it from a distance. Yes, it was one on their list.

It was Cyril who spotted the group of people up ahead and pulled into the stopping place as they waved him down. He wound down his window.

'Good morning, Sir. Western Country Customs here. We are doing a spot check on vehicles and documents.' The man had a pointy nose and flashed an official looking ID card. 'May I see your GoCards, please?'

At this point, neither Cyril nor Florence was concerned. If anything, they were impressed by the thoroughness of the excisers. Then Cyril saw the man shake his head, dislodging a drop of liquid off his nose and he grew worried.

'What is it?' he asked and found himself looking into the snout of a class A water pistol.

'Move over, Sir, and let me into the driving seat. It will be better for you and your lady wife if you don't make a fuss.'

The man climbed in as Cyril was forced into the back seat. Seconds later a panel opened in the side of the tunnel and the car disappeared into it. Then it closed, like

a predator's mouth over its prey and there was nothing to show that anyone had ever been there.

Well, almost nothing.

Captain Colin worked out like any hero should, for being in peak condition was vital for his work. He had done his ankle and knee exercises and was about to perform a small dragon slayer's dance, excellent for limbering up. His spark resistant stockings were a lovely shade of Justiciary Green.

But the insistent beep of his mobile telephonic device could not be ignored and, as he picked it up and listened into the ear piece, his expression became serious, then downright worried.

It was Auntie Gert and she was anxious. 'They should be here by now,' she said over and over again. 'I know they left on time because they called me from the terminal just before they took the tunnel.'

'OK Auntie Gert,' said Captain Colin. 'Let me check a couple of things out and I promise that I will call you back. There is probably a perfectly reasonable explanation for this.' His face, when he finished the call, was the very picture of determination, his kind eyes steely and his teeth glinting, even without sunlight.

Agent Ribbitt was hard at work running City Computer Checks (CCCs) on all vehicles using the tunnel. It was just one of the ways in which the Justiciary could check that they weren't letting any villains through to Western Country and Western Country were nice enough to provide the same service for traffic from their side.

She looked up as Captain Colin approached and gulped. 'Good morning, Captain. What can I do for you?'

'Hello, Agent Ribbitt,' he replied. 'I would like you to check that vehicle registration number CV1234 entered the tunnel this morning. Here is my authority to request this.' He placed a form on the table, with the official stamp. (This was important or else any old person could ring up and pretend they needed to check who had gone where).

She glanced at the form and entered the number into her computer. A sound like a whistle went off and up popped the answer.

'That vehicle entered the tunnel at 0645,' she confirmed and Captain Colin frowned. 'Is there a problem?'

'Have there been any reported accidents or people stopping too long for a picnic?'

We might smile but there had been several instances of families stopping in the tunnel and picnicking by candlelight, panicking other drivers and causing excisers no end of problems.

Again Agent Ribbitt scanned her computer and pressed some keys. Another noise like a whistle sounded and she shook her head. 'Normal running reported in both tunnels. Do you want me to alert the Western Country Excisers?'

Captain Colin nodded his assent and left the room. Agent Ribbitt picked up the phone to make the call she had promised. However, she did not make just one call, but two...

A call back to Auntie Gert did not make the situation any easier. Captain Colin was at his wits end. This was not just an ordinary disappearance; this was his family. In the end, he called Lt Quested to his office.

'I want you to lead the search for my parents, please,' he asked her. 'It's too personal for me, but I would still like to be involved.'

Lt Quested was just leaving to set up a team of agents and excisers, when another agent, Agent Khan, burst in without knocking, nearly sending Lt Quested flying like a bowling pin.

'Sorry, sorry,' Agent Khan apologised profusely. 'We have had word of a ransom letter that has come from a person or persons unknown, located in Western Country, about ten vehicles and their occupants, who have been captured.'

Further talks and a look at the letter confirmed that there had indeed been a series of kidnaps. The perpetrators were asking for ≠10,000 as a down payment (≠ is the symbol for the City's currency; crowns) with a further ≠40,000 in exchange for the poor people they had nabbed.

'There's a secret tunnel,' said Agent Khan excitedly. 'It's the only explanation. No traffic could go in and out of the tunnel undetected and no one can disappear into thin air without magic.'

Captain Colin and Lt Quested looked at each other. He had a point. Within minutes a team was assembled at both ends of the tunnel. They would enter and comb it goblin length by goblin length, to get clues. All other traffic was suspended and the tunnel shut, much to the annoyance of Witch Warble, who was on her way to attend a witches' reunion at the Pickled Frog Coven Centre in Western Country.

Elsewhere Cyril and Florence were sitting in a big low roofed building, in the sort of chairs you might find in a cinema, looking at a big white wall. There were about twenty people in all, confused and a little worried. Then a silhouette appeared and a most extraordinary sounding voice broke the silence.

'Greetings,' said the shadow, without waiting for a response. 'You are here to make me money. Do as you are told and you will come to no harm. If you try to be clever clogs, you will be shut in a small room. The choice is yours.'

No one moved a muscle. Everyone listened intently.

'We have asked for money for your safe return. Once this has been received, we will take you through a procedure of forgetfulness, so that you can't tell anyone what happened to you. This does not hurt - though some of the side effects include thinking you are a kangaroo or a beef burger. This does wear off. For now though, we wait.' And the silhouette disappeared, just like that.

Low murmuring broke out among the audience. Some comforted others, some sat in silence, praying that help would arrive. The minutes ticked by.

Checking every stopping place in the tunnel was a painstaking process, but at last it yielded a result. A blue scarf had been dropped at stopping point number 36, about three quarters of the way along the tunnel. Captain Colin, who was not in charge of but with the search team, pounced on it.

'It's my mother's,' he said. 'Mary and I bought it for her birthday. Good old Mum, she has left it as a clue. I knew there was no fire without dragon.' (You can probably see where Captain Colin gets some of his initiative from now).

They shone their torches over the tunnel area but could find nothing. Then, with a shout, Agent Khan motioned everyone to come across to where he was.

Imagine that the tunnel looks like a Swiss roll. At equidistant intervals, lines runs across and around it, like the line you might mark with a knife when you want to cut a slice. Well, what Agent Khan had discovered was a horizontal line running between two of these other lines, looking a bit like a giant H. This was right where the scarf had been dropped and this was, in all likelihood, the point where they had disappeared.

There was lots of information flying across the airwaves and structure technicians and drilling equipment were ordered from Western Country to come to stopping point number 36 in the tunnel. Understandably, people were very nervous. It's quite a big thing, to drill a hole in a tunnel under the sea. What if a passing shark decides to investigate and hasn't yet had its breakfast?

A worried Agent Ribbitt was on her other mobile telephonic device. 'I am telling you, Malcolm, I think they are onto us. I just intercepted some radiophonic dialogue and they have asked for drills to be taken into the tunnel.'

At the other end of the line, Malcolm was biting his nails. 'Well, they can't link the kidnaps to us. They have no proof. But you can't ring me again on your private device. You have to ditch it.' He rang off and Agent Ribbitt, thinking quickly, left her office.

At the same time as Auntie Gert's hair was exploding even more with worry and Mary and the children were waiting for news from Captain Colin, a structure technician had pronounced that there was a hollow on the other side of the concrete segment. They drilled gingerly, on the lookout for fish. When the first chunk of concrete caved in, Agent Khan stuck his head through the hole and shone his torch into the gloom. His expression when he came out again was incredulous.

'It's another tunnel,' he breathed. 'I was right. It's ingenious; a secret tunnel.'

More drilling took place and soon there was a gap wide enough to let people through. They advanced carefully, leaving the structure technicians to guard the hole.

They walked steadily upwards, the tunnel running along a gentle incline, until finally they reached a set of metal doors.

Lt Quested unfolded a roll of cloth which contained Justiciary lock and door panel picking tools. As well as being a very skilled Chima decoder, as you will see in the next story, she was also a level six lock breaker (there are only seven levels, the last being genius grade). There was complete silence and they did hear a pin drop when, nervous from all the tension, Lt Quested lost her skeleton key. Everyone jumped almost out of their boots!

There was a 'shushing' sound as the doors slid back and the team crept soundlessly through them into a corridor, lit by dim yellow lights. With Lt Quested leading and Captain Colin bringing up the rear, they walked uphill in single file towards a noise they could hear, like a machine talking.

Through a doorway, the most amazing scene met their eyes. A huge projection machine was whirring away and, just past it they could catch a glimpse of a shadow on the wall beyond. Seated in a chair, his feet up on a desk covered in sweet wrappers and reels of film, was a man with long dark hair, talking into a microphone with a synthesizer on it. The result was extraordinary. He sounded like an emergency vehicle siren, on two notes, relentless and ear splitting.

'We are still waiting for contact from the Justiciary,' he droned, clearly enjoying himself, 'so you will have the pleasure of my company a little while longer.'

As he went on, clearly loving the sound of his own voice, Lt Quested motioned some agents, led by Agent Khan, to creep into the auditorium. Then she, Captain Colin and one other exciser crept up on the man and tapped him on the shoulder.

He fell off his seat with fright and, while he was gently restrained, Lt Quested took the microphone. 'Please listen carefully,' she said slowly. 'At this very moment, Western Country and City agents are in the room with you. Everyone must remain where they are. Please do not move.'

Agent Khan found a light switch and threw it, revealing some very relieved and some very cross faces. Most of the people in the room were delighted to see the agents, but some people had just seen their dreams of big money disappear in the flick of a light switch. The team set about their business, escorting the villains back to Western Country Justiciary and taking statements from all of those who had been kidnapped.

Captain Colin hugged Florence and Cyril. 'I am so proud of you, Mum. We'll make an agent of you yet.'

It did not take long to round up the miscreants in the City. Malcolm told the agent taking his statement everything, chewing his fingertips as his nails had long since disappeared. It turned out that he was going out with Agent Ribbitt and, ambitious and impatient, they had seen a chance to make more money in one go than they might make in two years in their jobs.

The brains behind the scheme was a Western Country junior chess champion, Leopold Bishop, who had been a celebrity in his youth and rather liked it. When the attention dried up and no one wanted to know about a used-to-be-champion, he hatched a plan to play a big game of chess, using real people and scare tactics.

He created a chess expert website, which was really a front for a chat room where aspiring meanies could swap ideas for scams and schemes. Agent Ribbitt and Malcolm were frequent visitors to the site. Gradually, over a period of weeks, Leopold had drawn them into his net with the lure of easy money, in return for some low risk espionage.

He was unrepentant flicking his hair like a film star on the red carpet at a premiere. 'We had a plant in the ticket office in The City, who scanned the car registration numbers as people booked to use the tunnel and passed them to our plant in the Justiciary over there. Brilliant! I am a genius.'

'Except that you got caught,' pointed out the agent.

'Maybe,' he countered, 'but I corrupted an incorruptible agent.'

Some people just could not, or would not see the error of their ways. Leopold's boasting got him nothing more than a life sentence of teaching chess in primary schools and invigilating tournaments for free. To the end of his life, he remained unapologetic.

As for Agent Ribbitt, the worst thing was the expression on Captain Colin's face when he asked to see her.

'Agent Ribbitt,' he began sternly. 'You have disappointed me and your fellow colleagues more than I can possibly say. The safety of those innocent people was in your hands and you traded that for money. You are to leave the Justiciary and never return.'

Her head bowed, she put her Justiciary card and mobile telephonic device on the desk and, as she left, there were tears in her eyes.

Captain Colin twirled his moustache and thought. It had been a tough day. Then he picked up his mobile telephonic device, dialled a number and spoke into the mouthpiece.

'Yes hello, Auntie Gert. I'm just calling to say that Mum and Dad are fine. We will all come and stay soon, I promise.'

Well, even a dragon slayer deserves a holiday.

With an almost invisible click, the seventh piece of Captain Colin's heart docked perfectly. He thought it was his mobile telephonic device and, talking into the mouthpiece, spoke to his son and daughters and promised to be home soon.

Travail Eight: The Space Invaders

It was a lovely, clear night, perfect for star gazing and fishing, though perhaps not at the same time. On the far bank of the river, just outside the City, two night time anglers were enjoying the peace, the only sounds either their low voices or the fish rising to the surface of the water, rippling it and diving away again down to the bottom.

George Large, the father, took a sip of cold tea and relaxed in his chair. His rod was still and he rested his hand on it, waiting to detect the slightest movement. His son, George Little (they followed a traditional country practice of having the same first name and different last name), was just dozing off when something startled him.

Three dazzling shapes appeared in the sky. They shone like flattened disco balls but didn't spin. Instead they hung there eerily, twinkling and silent, blocking the stars. The Georges were petrified, stuck to their chairs and unable to make a sound. They stared at the gleaming dishes, which stared blankly back. There was no opening in their smooth surface; there were no windows or doors.

By the time the sun had risen, they were gone as quickly and as quietly as they had arrived. Now able to speak because the danger had passed, father and son puzzled over what they had seen.

'What do you think, George?' said George Large.

'I don't know, Dad,' said George Little.

Rather than alarm anyone in case they had imagined the whole thing, George and George opted to fish again the following night, with no cold tea and saw exactly the same thing again. The orbs arrived with speed and stealth, shining and silent, hanging in the sky. This time George and George were not alone and the streets were thronged with people gazing upwards and pointing at the shapes in the sky.

Their silence was menacing and, when the sun broke over the rim of the earth, the shapes disappeared, as if travelling faster than the speed of light.

It was the talk of the City. People gossiped in shops and offices, at school gates and over their fences. Some thought it was a trick of the light or atmospheric interference, but elsewhere something far more sinister, known only to a few souls, was unfolding.

A spoken letter had been a-mailed to the Justiciary that morning. Very few agents had ever heard of such a thing, let alone seen one. It was delivered immediately to Captain Colin.

'We need the 'Chima' and your skills,' he told Lt Quested, who rushed off immediately. She was one of a handful of agents who had studied the Chima as a special module in her agent training and had written a thesis on it.

The Chima machine looked a bit like a type writer but with a screen. It recognised different sound frequencies and matched them to letters of our alphabet. A spoken letter was always written in song format. First the decoder had to find the right key, then note the notes and finally substitute letters. This is not as easy as it sounds and is sometimes made more difficult if the creator of the letter a) can't sing or b) can't spell.

At last the encrypted sounds made sense. Lt Quested brought the resulting message straight to Captain Colin.

Dear Peeple of the planet City (it read, with some pretty poor spelling).

Wee have travelled many miles from the planet of Velouria, to anex your planet and use its resauces for ourselfs. Defianse is pointless. Wee will contact you again soon. Keep it hanging.

The Velouria Interplanetary Commission.

There was silence. Captain Colin and Lt Quested exchanged a long look.

'No mistake?' he asked.

'No mistake,' replied Lt Quested firmly and her boss nodded, his face serious.

Contact from other galaxies was not unknown even in these modern times, but it had <u>always</u> been in the spirit of exploration and knowledge sharing. This spoke of invasion and force. This was frightening.

In another part of the City, Jed and Honoria Tiberius were sitting in their lounge. One look told you that they were twins; both with thick dark hair and bright blue eyes and that they both shared the same incredibly bored expression. They came from one of the City's richest and most established families. In a democracy, they were the closest thing to nobility that the City's folks knew.

Their parents were philanthropists and art lovers, who had dedicated their lives to making their money work for them and for others. On the surface, Jed and Honoria appeared to be made of the same stuff.

But boredom is a funny thing with strange consequences. It had started with small dares, each egging the other on, to see what they could get away with and blame someone else. It had escalated from tricks to schemes and then to scheming. Right now they were composing something, their faces alight with laughter.

The second letter, decoded by Lt Quested, came about three days later. The spelling was just as bad and the tone much ruder.

Peeple of the planet City

Wee, The Velouria Interplanetary Commission, demand the furst payment of ≠100,000 to be maid by the mare today at miday. Do not deefalt or ourselfs will retaliate. Defianse is pointless. Leeve the money in the copse in the north sector.

The Velouria Interplanetary Commission

Despite the best efforts of the Justiciary to keep things quiet, news of the second letter had been leaked and the whole City was there to see Mayor Chillblain driving towards the north sector. He, Captain Colin and Lt Quested had been closeted for an hour, seeing if there was any way out of the predicament. They had agreed a secret plan, the first stage of which was to pay the money and keep the invaders sweet.

Mayor Chillblain entered the copse, which had so recently been in upheaval. He walked through the trees and left the bag under the oak tree. As he retreated, a figure watched him from behind another tree, a smile on her lips.

That evening, having put the children to bed and comforted Mary, Captain Colin was in his shed, tinkering with his lunar rocket. There was something about the first spoken letter from the Velourian Interplanetary Commission that teased the edges of his brain. He shook his head. Years of practice made him stop trying to fish for an answer, as it would come in its own sweet time.

The City was jittery. Life went on, but people were scared and a second monetary payment was to be made to the Velourians. Every night those noiseless vessels hovered in the inky sky, their silent menace exerting a powerful hold over the populous. It was believed that their ships had weapons and no one wanted to find out what would happen if they were used.

Captain Colin felt powerless and it was not a nice experience. He had never before been faced with a problem that he couldn't resolve within a short space of time. Although the first stage of the plan, agreed with Mayor Chillblain, had been to give the invaders their ransom money, two payments had now been made and the overt surveillance work had revealed nothing. Night after night agents in bushes had had their infrared binofocular lenses (or 'biffs' as they were known - the very latest thing in night vision technology) trained on the ships, trying vainly to spot creatures going in or out, or to work out where the ships disappeared to so suddenly when morning came.

It was a complete mystery.

On the same day that the third spoken letter was delivered to Lt Quested and she began her decoding work, two very important events occurred.

The first involved preparations for the grand reopening of the City Laser Palace, through money donated by the Tiberius Foundation, run by Jed and Honoria's parents. It had been closed for some time, as city money went to other projects and, more recently, into the Velourian state purse. However, the funds had been found and hundreds of children were looking forward to laser parties and competitions again. Now the scaffolding was shifted and the carpets cleaned ahead of the evening's entertainment.

The second involved George Little.

The night before the third spoken letter arrived at the Justiciary, George was watching the ships through his bedroom window. He felt angry at their presence. What right did they have to block his view of the stars? He hadn't been fishing since that second night, too spooked by them to risk going out of the City to the river. He suddenly leapt up and, crossing his room, rummaged in his wardrobe. What he pulled out was a pellet pistol.

Even though he knew he was breaking the rules agreed with his parents about the use of his pellet pistol, George was too cross to care. He didn't have a plan, but let himself silently out of the house and made his way down the deserted streets to the edge of the City and into the fields beyond.

He stopped, put down his bag, drew two luminous pellets out of it and loaded his pellet pistol. Then, before taking aim at the nearest ship, he raised his fist and shook it angrily.

'Who do you think you are?' he shouted at the silent discs. 'Coming here and stopping folk from doing what they want to do. Get lost!' With that he took aim and fired at the nearest ship to him.

Those luminous pellets, travelling at the speed of $\sum = \sqrt{(34\frac{3}{4}x\frac{7}{8}\boxtimes)^4}$, traced a visible line to the nearest ship. George waited, barely breathing, to hear the impact...but there was nothing; no clang, or zap. They seemed to pass straight through the nearest ship. He tried again with the same result.

Why didn't the ship have a protective force field around it? Why had the pellets been allowed to pierce its outer surface? Why hadn't anyone shouted 'ouch'? Puzzled and aware that it was very late, George made his way back home.

On the day of the reopening of the City Laser Palace George sat in Captain Colin's office with his dad, nervous and tongue tied. Captain Colin smiled at him.

'George, why don't you tell me all about your adventure?' he asked and George did.

Something flickered in Captain Colin's mind; a wisp of an idea; a hint of a resolution to the problem of the

Velourian ships. He had always thought it strange that no one had actually seen a Velourian. Perhaps they were very shy.

Or perhaps not.

'Still,' he thought. 'There's no fire without dragon.'

The City welcomed the festival atmosphere that accompanied the grand reopening of the City Laser Palace. It was quite oppressive being invaded and people were glad of a chance to let off steam. Lights were strung from the lamp posts and a spectacular firework display would take place later. Maybe that would force a few Velourians to decamp!

The silent ships hovered as row upon row of cars drew up, decanting their elegant and bejewelled occupants onto the red carpet, as flash bulbs popped and people cheered. Mr and Mrs Tiberius waved and signed programmes, followed by Jed and Honoria, whose smiles didn't quite reach their eyes. There was to be an opening ceremony during which Mrs Tiberius would cut a ribbon and say a few words and Mr Tiberius would demonstrate a laser racquet.

A laser was beamed from the handle of the racquet, deflected with the racquet head and lobbed back towards the person's opponent. It was great family fun. All Jed and Honoria had to do was look on, smile and clap.

All of this jolliness was then to be followed by a stunning *son et lumiere* show, depicting Captain Colin vanquishing the dragon from travail four of our story.

For this special occasion Captain Colin was in his most regal stockings, which had drawn gasps of admiration from the crowd. As he listened to the speech made by Mrs Tiberius, he turned and said a few words to Jed, who was playing the role of the attentive son to perfection.

'You must be very proud of your parents, Jed.'

'Of course' replied Jed, turning to look at Captain Colin.

'Mary and I are going to take our places for the show now. Perhaps we'll catch one another later?'

'Sure,' said Jed absently. 'Keep it hanging, Captain.'

As the conversation finished, something slotted into place for Captain Colin and he settled down to watch the show, Mary at his side.

He was in work so early the next morning that the ships were still just visible and he woke the sparrows. Going through the first letter decoded by the Chima machine, he read and re-read one phrase. Then, with a smile and a silent message of thanks to whoever was listening, he picked up his mobile telephonic device and summoned Lt Quested.

It was a discreet line of cars that drove out to the Tiberius mansion later that morning. At Captain Colin's request the whole family had gathered in the salon together with Mayor Chillblain. Captain Colin looked at each and every one of them sternly, before addressing them. Honoria shifted in her seat slightly, an anxiety tummy ache starting in the pit of her stomach.

'Mr Tiberius, you possess a Chima machine, do you not?' asked Captain Colin.

Mr Tiberius nodded. 'Yes – I have always been interested in intergalactic memorabilia. It's one of only three in existence that I know of.'

Jed looked bored and Honoria worried.

'And your children understand how to work it?' Captain Colin continued his questioning.

Again Mr Tiberius nodded. Jed now looked a little less bored and Honoria was white.

Captain Colin explained how, the previous evening, Jed had finished their conversation with a trendy phrase 'keep it hanging.' This had been the same phrase used in the first spoken letter and it had seemed so out of place in a ransom demand. This, plus the incident with George Little's luminous pellets, has provided the breakthrough for the Justiciary. Captain Colin had put two and two together and had come up with the square root of sixteen.

'How did you do it?' he asked Jed, who just shrugged. 'Honoria?' She spoke in a torrent of words, like racing water.

They had discovered the secret by accident, she explained, while running through a book of blue magic (spells which are both evil and rude). They discovered that, by clever use of light and mirrors, they could set up holographic images of whatever they wanted, by projecting a single image onto lots of reflective surfaces. On a small scale it was scary enough, but they were thinking of the bigger picture. How could they use this technology to scare the people of the City into parting with their wealth?

Then Honoria had unearthed a book about the planet Velouria, which was pure fiction, but which would give them the story they needed to start their plan.

Finally, it was Jed's fascination with the Chima machines (his father had his on display in his study), that brought all the pieces of the dastardly jigsaw together.

The Tiberius family owned a lot of buildings (called real estate) in the City. With a crew of horrid accomplices, Jed and Honoria coated the solar panels on all of their buildings and outbuildings with reflective paint. This sent a single image of a spaceship bouncing into the night sky, so that a picture of a ship became an army of hovering, silent vessels.

Jed laughed. 'It was so simple. People are such dimwits.'

Honoria had the grace to look ashamed at the disgust she saw in her parents' faces.

'Jed, Honoria,' their mother cried. 'We brought you up to know better than this.'

'Mother, dear, you brought us up to be useless accessories for you and father. It's so tiresome being nice all the time. A little malice is good for the soul.' Jed drawled, hanging his leg over the sofa, any shame noticeably absent.

'I will ask you both to leave the room, please,' requested Captain Colin, 'while I speak with the Mayor and your parents about this crime. Lt Quested, please remain with them.'

'I am sorry,' whispered Honoria, as she left the room.

'I'm not – and I know my rights and stuff,' shouted Jed defiantly.

The discussion was brief and to the point. Sentencing in the City was based on redemptive rightdoing, to achieve three things:

1. A good outcome for the persons affected by the wrongdoing
2. A suitable redemptive rightdoing programme for the wrongdoers
3. Value added to the community through number two.

Justice swiftly took its course and Jed and Honoria were sentenced to live at home for five years and each work in a hostel for the homeless, without a penny being paid to them. Honoria threw herself into her programme, but time dragged for Jed at roughly the same speed as he dragged his feet in his programme!

That evening, the City rejoiced that the shadowy ships had gone and toasted Captain Colin and Mayor Chillblain again and again, under bright stars and a full moon. Some felt sad that the Tiberius parents had such ungrateful children. It was noted that Captain Colin had not had to perform an aeronautical miracle to achieve his outcome, but then, it had involved space ships.

Sitting out under the stars with Mary, Christopher, Alison and Bea, Captain Colin felt completely at peace. Softly, like a key turning in a lock, the eighth piece of his heart clicked into place and all was right with the world.

Travail Nine: Captain Colin Makes a Mistake

It was a chilly evening and little fingers of mist curled around car tyres and people's ankles as they walked. Just outside the city limits on the river, a boat named 'The Mermaid' had berthed, waiting for customs excisers to check that its papers and cargo were in order. Excisers were being particularly vigilant since they had received some intelligence that there was an increase in snuggling activity. Snuggling is like smuggling, but the people are a bit nicer.

The crew, a mixture of men and women, sat talking as their Commander, Florentina Blunderbuss, kept a watchful eye on the Exciser Office. She could see people moving about, chatting and shuffling papers. She hated this bit – the waiting. It made her nervous. She pulled her coat about her broad frame and tucked her grey hair behind her ears.

Over in the Exciser Office, excisers were reviewing their lists. Checking the boats was a lengthy process and there were two to do before they got to 'The Mermaid.'

Captain Colin had woken up early with a bounce in his step and a tingle in his cheek, which could mean toothache. Today he was reviewing progress at the Soccer Academy he had founded years before and he loved these visits. The club house and pitches were well maintained and the five squads were out training; three for boys and two for girls. He watched them go through their exercises and spoke with the coaches about the progress of each player.

After training Captain Colin met with the boys and girls in the squads, motivating them with his interest and firing them up to do well for him and for themselves. Christopher was in boys' squad two.

'I am proud of you all,' said Captain Colin to the eager faces in front of him. 'You are showing great prowess. Good luck in the intercity league tournament. I shall come to as many matches as I can.'

Herb Garden was there; you might remember him as the shadow stealer from travail one. He looked and felt like a completely different person. Gone was the sullen face and the poor attitude, to be replaced by a smiling sports fanatic with some pretty nifty keepie uppie skills.

Captain Colin left the academy that afternoon. He felt a twinge in his cheek, as though the toothache were saying 'hello'. Impatiently, he ignored it; there was too much work to do.

As night fell in the City a very ardent and new customs exciser was vigilantly scanning the customs area. There were a dozen or so boats moored there, all waiting for the necessary checks. Most of them were in darkness, their crews bedded down for the night, or at least until the excisers came knocking. Exciser Marshall's attention fell on 'The Mermaid'. It was lit up like a giant glow worm, tatters of mist floating eerily by.

She peered through the gloom. There was frantic activity on board. Although too far away to see the details of what they were doing, Exciser Marshall could see some crates and lots of objects on the deck. While it was not unusual to see activity on a boat, some sixth sense (which would make her a truly excellent exciser and a future head of the Justiciary) made her want to investigate further. Grabbing her 'biffs, she switched off the office light and watched what was happening, undetected.

Just after nightfall Captain Colin was in the grip of the worst toothache he had ever known. A day out of the office had meant piles of paperwork to catch up on and he had elected to work late to get it done. He had sent a goodnight a-mail to his children and Mary and received one of Bea's poems in return.

ꙅꙅꙩꙅ

Hey, Dad, I'm pretty rapt in
The fact that you're the Captain
Of the Justiciary
You're a hard working father
But you know I would far rather
That you were home for tea.
Love you, Dad.
See you l8er. xx

He tried to smile, but his cheek was frozen in pain. Two aspirin, an ancient chant, a clove of cinnamon and some herbal tea had not helped him. The pain made all the nerve endings in his left jaw and ear jingle jangle.

Back at the river, Exciser Marshall was sure that the crew on 'The Mermaid' were up to something. Florentina Blunderbuss was standing with her feet apart, waving her hands around and the crew were scrabbling around on the deck, moving what appeared to be kitchen implements from one crate to another. There was straw everywhere.

Exciser Marshall put down her 'biffs' and, using her super subtle torch, checked the papers about ship's cargo.

Item	Quantity	Unit price (≠)
Wooden bowls (sustainable source)	4000	6.75
Wooden spoons (sustainable source)	10000	2.93

She read the list (you can only see a fraction of it here). Then she focused her 'biffs' on the boat again. What in the galaxy was going on?

When the call came through on his mobile telephonic device from Exciser Marshall, Captain Colin was less than his usual alert self. He was sitting in his chair, trying not to move his head, because each time he did so his nerve endings jangled like an out of tune orchestra. He picked up his device.

'Captain Coli-,' he said with difficulty.

'Sir,' said Exciser Marshall, 'it's the Exciser Office here. I am calling to report some unusual activity aboard one of the boats waiting for customs clearance. I have been watching them for some time. Earlier on I could see the crew unpacking crates and packing them again. It seems completely illogical, Captain. I would like to recommend that we conduct a random night search, with aerial tracking.'

Captain Colin groaned in pain, but 'oooh eeeh' sounds a lot like 'ok' over a crackling telephonic line. Exciser Marshall took his groan to mean agreement.

'Right oh, Captain. I'll give the order for the ground search to be to organised, if you can get the Pied Piper Hamlin scrambled. I'll meet you here in one hour.' She hung up.

Captain Colin winced as he dialled the number for the air crew.

'Thi- i- Captai- Coli-,' he said through a mouth that was now completely numb on one side, thanks to the herbal tea. However, it was the wrong side. So now, as well as excruciating toothache, he could hardly pronounce his words.

'-cramble the play.'

The agent who took the call checked that Captain Colin wanted the plane scrambled and was answered with an '-es'. Later he said that he just thought it was a bad line.

To make things look quite normal, Exciser Marshall and her team had already conducted one search on another boat and were preparing to board 'The Mermaid'. There were some additional excisers waiting on the dock for her signal, in case things got tricky and she was waiting for sight or sound of Captain Colin.

Suddenly she heard the comforting drone of the aircraft engines and signalled a 'thumbs up' to her fellow excisers.

They swarmed over the boat, under the baleful stare of Florentina, checking crew, papers and crates. She remained where she was, her eyes flicking from the excisers to her crew and back.

'Don't panic,' her eyes said. 'Make like a clam and keep your mouths shut.'

The crates that were opened contained articles of kitchenware from sustainable sources. The excisers didn't burrow too far down into them, as they knew that an infrared sweep of the vessel was imminent.

Sandwiched between the night sky and the boat, Captain Colin swept the decks with the Pied Piper's optimum infrared 'biffs', barely able to think straight and groaning with discomfort. This reduced his concentration levels by approximately 37.67565% and increased the margin for error by a disproportionately proportionate amount.

The setting on the 'biffs' meant that anything that wasn't wood would glow green instead of white. This included all humans and any rats who had stowed on board without so much as a 'by your leave'. Ordinarily Captain Colin would have picked up any anomaly in the reading on his screen, but he was simply unable to do anything except try not to scream in agony.

Consequently the search revealed nothing. Exciser Marshall was left questioning her sixth sense and Captain Colin went home to bed, in the grip of the worst toothache ever. Florentina Blunderbuss and her crew celebrated with extra blackcurrant juice and raisin rations.

'I don't understand it,' whispered Exciser Marshall to herself. 'I was so sure.'

'Don't worry,' said her boss. 'Better to make the call and find nothing than to do nothing and let a gang of snugglers go free.'

It didn't make her feel any better.

It was a week later that the storm broke over Captain Colin's head. When the crates were delivered to the City's kitchen emporium, they were found to contain a top layer of wooden kitchen implements, and then three layers of plastic ones. We already know that the 'biffs' picked up on this by a slight variance in colour, but Captain Colin had missed this.

Now sales were down at the kitchen emporium, the market was flooded with poor quality kitchenware and the crew of 'The Mermaid' had pocketed a fortune that wasn't theirs. The people of the City looked at one another and shook their heads.

'You can't even trust the resident hero to do the job right. What is the world coming to?' they asked.

MAYOR CHILLBLAIN CALLS A COMMISSION OF ENQUIRY screamed the City Chronicle headlines. This was to hold Captain Colin and the customs excisers to account.

Captain Colin was at home on the morning that the commission of enquiry was due to start. He sat on the bed and sighed. Mary frowned, hating to see him so forlorn. She gave him a hug and a pep talk.

'Listen to me, CC,' she said, looking him in the eye. 'You are in for a tough time today. You have to tell them the truth. All those who really know you believe in you and will support you. I'll be there and your critics will have me to deal with. Now wear your uniform and be proud, darling.'

The court room was packed to the rafters, with those ranging from well wishers to nosey parkers. Imagine a court room, if you can. Mayor Chillblain sat where the judge would normally be, and either side of him sat two other commissioners.

It was a long and tedious process. Exciser Marshall was questioned at some length about the night's events. She gave her evidence in a calm, clear voice and, when she was done, shot a sympathetic look at Captain Colin, which he returned with a slight smile. She had only told the truth.

Having heard from the other witnesses, Mayor Chillblain summoned Captain Colin to the stand. A whisper ran like a ripple round the room. This was what the crowd had waited for – a glimpse of their ex-hero. Mary squared her shoulders and willed Captain Colin to find the words he needed to say what he needed to say. She could only look on, love and disbelief written all over her face.

As he took the stand there was an audible gasp, for the Captain was a shadow of his former self. His eyes were dull, his cheeks pale and his left jaw was a little swollen, where he had had a tooth extracted the day before.

'Captain Colin,' began the Mayor, in his best television courtroom drama voice, stressing every other word like a television reporter, 'you are charged with neglecting to

carry out your duties to the best of your abilities on the night in question. What do you say to that?'

Captain Colin thought for a moment. The silence grew and grew until it became a loud noise. Then he spoke in a quiet, calm voice and people strained to catch his words. What would he say? What could he say?

'You, the people of this City, elected me as the guardian of your safety a long time ago. Until today, I have enjoyed your affection and admiration, but all this has been called into question.

'It is true that I omitted to distinguish the colour variation between the wooden and plastic goods on board 'The Mermaid' that night. We find ourselves here today as a direct consequence of my mistake.' He paused for breath and looked directly at the Mayor.

'Is it not also true that, despite my requests for funding to train other pilots, this has been denied, leaving me the only agent in the entire Justiciary able to fly the Pied Piper Hamlin?'

The crowd gasped and the Mayor went as red as his nose.

'I went to work at six o'clock on the morning in question. After spending all day at the Soccer Academy I stayed late at the office to complete some paperwork, all the while in the grip of a terrible toothache, which my dentist can confirm. If I had had a choice, people of the City, I would have suggested that the search take place another night.' He stopped, to take a sip of water.

The onlookers waited on tenterhooks for what he would say next.

'But you have made me your hero and a hero cannot be ill or refuse to take action if a crime is being committed. A hero is expected to fight through the pain and achieve the impossible. Let me tell you that this is tiring. I have never asked you to endow me with superhuman characteristics, but you have. And now, when you discover that I am human, you seek to bring me down.

'Others fail and are pardoned. I am not asking to avoid accountability for my actions. I am asking for you to see me as I really am and not as you would wish me to be.'

There was uproar in the courtroom. There was applause, shouting, cheering and general pandemonium. A small group of cheerleaders sprang to their feet holding up letters that spelled out:

G-O C-A-P-T-A-I-N C-O-L-I-N

Then Captain Colin held up his hands.

'I have played my part in keeping this City safe and perhaps it is time for me to move over and let younger, fresher eyes and ears take the lead. Mayor Chillblain, you will have my resignation on your desk tomorrow morning.' He left the stand, the room and the building without looking back.

The outbursts of support which followed were sensational. Captain Colin received a-mails, calls, letters and flowers. He sat in his office, his head in his hands, full of despair for what he had done, but ready to face the consequences.

Love is a very important thing. When we love someone, we allow them to be who they really are and help them if they want to change. When we are loved, we are free to be who we are, too. This is important because it was as though the whole City had been wearing rose tinted glasses through which they saw Captain Colin.

Now the lenses in those glasses had been replaced by clear glass and they could see him for what he really was. And they loved him all the more because of it.

When the Commission of Enquiry reconvened the following week, it was to rule that Captain Colin would receive a suspended suspension of one day, remain as Head of the Justiciary and receive funding for a leadership academy. There was more cheering and clapping. Mary had tears in her eyes as she smiled at her husband.

Exciser Marshall came to see Captain Colin in his office later that day. 'Are you busy, Captain?'

'Not too busy to see you, Exciser Marshall. Come in and have some tea with me. You have some news, I think.'

'I have come to thank you, Captain. I have been asked to head up a team to work with the Intercity Justiciary to bring the crew of 'The Mermaid' to justice and recover the stolen money.' Her blue eyes sparkled with excitement.

'You deserve it,' smiled Captain Colin.

'I am sure that you had something to do with it,' insisted Exciser Marshall, but Captain Colin simply sipped his tea and said nothing.

After she had gone, he remembered an old dragon slayer motto. 'There is no fire without dragon.' Well, Exciser Marshall was off to find her dragon and he had certainly just slain the biggest dragon of his life, in that courtroom.

That evening, one tooth and much pain lighter, Captain Colin sat in his sitting room and looked round at his family. They had always known who he really was, he thought, and with them he could be just himself.

The moon sailed over an ash coloured sky. The stars twinkled faintly in the distance, sprinkling a kind of magic dust over everything.

In its trailer, Captain Colin's heart came one step closer to being complete.

TRAVAIL TEN: MAJOR MAELSTROM MEETS HIS MATCH

Although he was unaware of it, Captain Colin was nearly at the end of a very important personal journey. His heart was almost complete. However, between him and the end of his journey lay one final, dreadful challenge...

If you are not easily scared, read on.

In a parallel universe, in a well lit, comfortable office (anti-heroes don't always hang around in the dark) sat a man. He was taller than any pygmy, shorter than any giant and stood shoulder to shoulder with any other man. He was brave, reckless even, once killing two dragons in the same afternoon.

His moustache was neatly trimmed; his stockings of impeccable quality and his eyes glinted. On his desk was a sign and it read:

Major Maelstrom:
Head of the Injusticiary

Once upon a time he had been a top Justiciary agent, performing amazing feats of derring do and with a glittering future ahead of him. Though worryingly prone to fits of arrogance and self-love, he had always achieved the right result and the City loved him. Women trembled when he smoothed his moustache and men wanted to be like him.

In his leadership tests he had scored the highest ever marks for; cunning, dissembling, fibbing, plotting and downright horridness. This score + reckless bravery = no heart!

One afternoon, while on a routine patrol of the west sector, Agent Maelstrom, as he was then, had interrupted a snatching operation. Miniature dragons, bred illegally by specialists, were trained to target members of the public, nip their arms causing them to drop their purses and wallets and fly away with their bounty. Catching one of the small dragons, he had tickled it until claws retracted and put it on a see through lead (agents always carry dragon leads).

Bouncing ahead of him on the air, with the imminent threat of more tickles, it led him down dark alleyways to a deserted depot just outside city limits. Inside, an astonishing sight met his eyes. Piles and piles of money were stacked under polythene sheets.

A sound made Maelstrom spin round and he came face to face with a wizened old crone in a long brown cloak. She seemed to know who he was; in fact you could almost say she had been expecting him.

'Please take a seat, Agent Maelstrom,' she offered in a cracked voice.

'How do you know my name?' He was curious, but unafraid.

119

'I have been expecting you a long time. My name is Chlorenia and you are here to get rich.'

When a corruptible person comes face to face with a corrupting opportunity, there is a double resistance to truth and so it was that Agent Maelstrom and Chlorenia began to talk.

'I know you,' he said. 'Didn't you used to do birth predictions with an abacus? You gave my mother some stupid poem about my nemeses or something.'

She nodded. 'Those twits could never pay me what I was worth, so I studied a few other money making ventures and here I am. As for the poems, they are not stupid. You have a great future ahead of you. Is your heart dark enough, I wonder?'

'Who or what is my nemesis?' he asked with a gleam in his eye.

Chlorenia smiled, showing a total of three teeth, like small black stumps. 'Stick with me,' she cackled, 'and all will be revealed.'

As it was, another agent rumbled his trickery and Agent Maelstrom was stripped of his agent status and banned from the City. He had founded the Injusticiary, using his ill gotten gains and Chlorenia's murky skills. It matched the Justiciary agent for agent, skill for skill, but was run on fear and darkness, instead of truth and trust. For every wrong that the Justiciary righted, the Injusticiary launched another caper.

That agent had been Captain Colin.

Now, back in the present Major Maelstrom was finessing a very cunning revenge plan. A lifetime's study of Captain Colin had led Major Maelstrom to the conclusion that the most important thing in the Captain's life was his family.

'So,' he whispered aloud to himself. 'I hurt you as much as you hurt me. This has been a long time coming, but the wait will have been worth it.'

Back in the City things were going through smoothly. The Leadership Academy was flourishing and Colin was in full health. He had recently attended a preliminary class for slayers of large dragons and had been delighted at his own progress.

The latest overt surveillance mission had been a success and another two members of the Laughing Gas Gang had been caught. It was a time to feel good.

The nightmare began on a Tuesday, after Captain Colin had dropped the children off at school. He smiled as Bea skipped in with her friends, turning to wave as she did so. He noted with a wry smile how different it was with the twins, who didn't want to be seen with their parent in front of their friends, even if that parent was a hero.

Alison and Christopher parted company in the main hall and went off to start their lessons.

The first hint of trouble came when Alison arrived home without her brother. This was not unusual but Tuesday was instrument practice day, with all three children expected home for an hour of music practice.

Mary was in the kitchen when Alison appeared. 'Hello, love. Where are Chris and Bea?'

'Bea has got her nose stuck in a book and I haven't seen Chris,' Alison replied, making herself a sandwich. 'Right, I'm off to get started.'

An hour went by with no word from Chris and Mary began to get cross, rather than worried. Then, at work, an a-mail bounced into Captain Colin's machine. It read:

Hello.
If you wish to see your son alive again,
then await further instructions.
TTFN (ta ta for now)
MM

Captain Colin stared at the screen and blinked. His colleague popped her head round the door.

'The Mayor is here to see you.'

Captain Colin rose to meet the Mayor, his mind whirling like a fast dragon dance. They had to co-sign a new charter for the City, a matter of just a few minutes. Captain Colin then made small talk with Mayor Chillblain, giving absolutely nothing away. The meeting over, he asked not to be disturbed drew a deep breath and checked his screen again. There was a second message.

Very good, it read.
Now go home, as your family needs you
Ciao for now.
MM

MM – Major Maelstrom!

As he opened his front door, Captain Colin could hear crying. His heart sank. This was no hoax. Even before Mary opened her mouth, her face told the whole story. The same a-mail had been sent to her at the same time. Captain Colin hugged her and promised that everything would be alright. Then he told his wife and daughters that no one must know what was happening.

After that he sat back and waited. No one could sleep.

It was midnight when the third message came.

Your son is safe. You for him; a straight swap.
Car outside.
MM

Captain Colin sent a one word response and then said what might be his last goodbyes to his family. He hugged his daughters and kissed his wife, accepting their protestations but firm in his decision and stepped out into the inky night.

In the driveway stood Christopher, pale but calm. He walked in a wobbly line towards his Dad, running the last three steps and hurling himself into his arms. Captain Colin hugged him fiercely and then told him to go on inside. He then walked towards the gate, where a sleek black car opened its door like a mouth waiting to swallow its prey.

Inside, the seats were of black leather and a smoked screen meant that Captain Colin could not see or communicate with the driver. In front of him, a small screen set into the seat flickered into life.

'Hello, Captain,' said Major Maelstrom. 'Well done. Good plan. See you in about, ooh, an hour.'

The image faded and Captain Colin stared out into the night, his face unreadable.

At length the car drew up outside a low, military style building long outside the city perimeter. It was painted metallic black. They entered via a sliding door and walked into a vast atrium, all glass and chrome and there, in that vast canopied space, he came face to face with...

'Major Maelstrom,' said Captain Colin. 'I suppose I must thank you for returning my son.'

The Major laughed. 'It was easy to snatch him from outside the school gates and take him. He is so full of trust, like his father, that he never expected the agents who approached him to be bad. Oh I outrank you, Captain, on every level. I have waited for this day, waited to pit my wits against yours and let the void prevail. I have lined up an eventful night for you. First a battle with a large dragon and, if you succeed, then a fight to the death with me.

'Of course the only death will be yours. Oh how the City will mourn the loss of their irreplaceable hero. They will be inconsolable and, just at that point, I will make them an offer they can't refuse.' He smiled and it wasn't pleasant. 'TTFN, my friend.'

'The truth will prevail, Maelstrom.' Captain Colin's voice was quiet in that big space.

'Truth?' spat Major Maelstrom, turning back to face his prisoner. 'The only truth tonight is your destruction and my triumph. Take him away.'

And so it was that Captain Colin found himself in a large floodlit cave, with ringside seats, all full of Injusticiary agents keen to witness the fall of a hero. A floor to ceiling wall of reinforced glass ran around the edge of the oval arena, separating the spectators from the action, cutting off any possible means of escape. The plumes of fire and smoke he could see from behind giant gates of galvanised steel at one end indicated a large-ish and hungry dragon.

Captain Colin had been given the choice of a single weapon and now held in his hand a long pointy sword. He stood alone in the middle of the arena, with steel gates locked behind him and steel gates opening in front of him.

From behind their screen, the audience caught their collective breath as the dragon advanced into the arena. It was fully thirty feet in height, covered in a mixture of brown and green scales, its wings folded behind it and its powerful tail twitching from side to side, sending stones and moss flying.

The dragon, kept in the dark and not properly fed for days, was dazzled by the flood lights (it is well documented that dragons have poor eyesight and need time to adjust to any changes in light). It could smell food, the scent of a tasty human assailing its nostrils. It raised its head and gave a terrifying roar, which sent all the agents in the audience back at least one row of seats.

The dragon could just about make out Captain Colin, who was fixed to the floor praying and, beyond it, another dragon; an ugly brute swaying from side to side. Two dragons and only one prey would not do. This interloper had to be dispatched. The dragon lifted its great head and shot a plume of smoke and flame from its nostrils into the air somewhere above Captain Colin's head. Then, like an earthquake with feet, it lumbered forward, picking up speed and headed blindly for...its reflection in the gates behind Captain Colin.

Having assessed in those short moments what was about to happen (dragons will always attack one another first) Captain Colin uttered a prayer and stood stock still, the blade of his sword pointing upwards above his head and angled to the right. The dragon ran towards him, its belly low to the ground, all fire and smoke and snatching jaws. But it swerved to avoid him and blundered towards what it thought was the other dragon.

As it did so, it conveniently ran to the right and Captain Colin hooked the point of the sword into its soft underbelly with deadly accuracy. The dragon felt a jab but was powerless to stop its forward momentum and Captain Colin ran the sword blade along the entire length of its tummy.

The dragon eventually stopped, looked down, looked at Captain Colin and keeled over. He dodged its great bulk just in time and watched as it fell and exploded into dragon dust. This is another important fact about dragons; they disperse into lots of tiny particles. The arena and its occupants were suddenly coated in a thin layer of green dust.

Captain Colin barely had time to catch his breath and retrieve the sword before there was a crackling sound, like a speaker revving up.

'You were lucky,' came Major Maelstrom's voice through the intercom. 'Now prepare to meet your end.'

The Major emerged from the same end of the arena as the dragon, covered in some green dust like an ancient warrior daubed with woad and doing a victory dance. It involved elaborate moustache twirling, while pirouetting and looking very fierce. The audience oohed and aahed.

Captain Colin was desperately tired. He had just vanquished a large dragon (anything over 25 feet is officially large according to the almanack) and he did not know if he would ever see his family again.

He brandished his sword, every muscle in his body aching and Major Maelstrom laughed as he jumped and twirled closer still. The intricate steps of his dance made his feet move faster than a hummingbird's wings. Closer and closer he drew to the Captain, mesmerising the onlookers.

Captain Colin had suffered from cramp as a boy. Even in adulthood, it afflicted him when he was tired and hadn't drunk enough water. A sudden pain shot up his leg making his toes curl and his muscles contract. It was so unexpected and painful that, without thinking, he straightened his leg, stretching it out in front of him and bent over to massage his calf.

Just at the moment that he bent over, Major Maelstrom was preparing to lunge forward with his sword. The Captain's impromptu movement wrong footed him and instead of hitting his enemy, he lost his balance, tripped over Captain Colin's outstretched foot and fell nose first to the ground. His weapon clattered on the sand, some distance away from him.

Immediately, Captain Colin turned him over, placed his foot on the Major's chest and pointed his sword at his head. He looked down into the Major's eyes, alight with hatred and the pain of a bruised nose. Captain Colin uttered an incantation and then everything went dark.

What happened to Major Maelstrom and how Captain Colin got back home is a mystery too great to be revealed in this book. But rest assured that the Major was put beyond the reach of any more trouble causing and Captain Colin drew up outside his house in the same car that had whisked him away earlier that night.

The birds were singing and a light blue line edged the horizon as he turned his key in the lock. Mary was sitting on the stairs and she flew into Captain Colin's open arms, crying and laughing and getting covered in dragon dust.

'You're all green,' she smiled, as she wiped away the streaks from his face with her hand.

Then the children came bouncing down the stairs with cries of, 'Dad, Dad!' They hugged him all at once, especially Christopher.

Later, they would talk about trust and observation. Christopher had taken it on trust that the two agents were from the Justiciary because they said that they were. He had not asked to see their cards. But right now, they sat side by side on the sofa, father and son, like peas in a pod.

Captain Colin sat down with his family that evening for tea. As he watched them chat and talk, his heart swelled with pride and thanks and the tenth piece of his heart slotted silently into place.

In its trailer, the lunar rocket was very excited. It had the feeling that, quite soon, it was going to be completed. Its rivets shook with anticipation and its engine revved even without any key in its ignition.

Later, his hands covered in oil from his work Captain Colin reflected that a true heart + luck = being a hero.

And if he can be a hero, so can we all.

Epilogue: A Full Heart

Captain Colin went down to the shed, where his heart lay partly assembled, with an old radio and a flask of tea. Working harder than he had ever worked before, Captain Colin succeeded in assembling all the bits of the lunar rocket.

Back in the house his family, complete and happy, went about their usual tasks. Christopher was watching telly with Bea, while Alison was on the phone to a friend, describing some well trendy shoes she was going to buy. Mary, overhearing the conversation from the kitchen, smiled to herself. She looked through the window at the shed, where her husband was tinkering with who knew what.

The smell of a freshly baked ginger cake wafted through the house and, as it tickled the children's noses and made their mouths water, they came into the kitchen one by one. Mary cut them each a slice.

'Mum, you are a miracle cake maker,' mumbled Bea through a mouth full of crumbs.

'I'd better have Dad's slice,' Christopher announced, having polished off a giant sized piece in two minutes flat. 'He won't know it's gone.'

Alison perched on her chair, elbows on the table, eating her cake slowly and with care. Mary watched her with a smile on her face. The speed at which Alison ate was a standing family joke.

'Dad will have his slice when he's ready,' she said gently. 'He'll be hungry after all that concentration.'

Tasty though it was, the smell of the cake didn't float right the way through the kitchen door and into the garden beyond. It didn't deter our hero from his work in the shed, as his hammer clanged and his screw driver squeaked.

It was dark and starry when he emerged, his kind eyes grimed with tiredness, his hands and nails filthy with oil. But he saw and felt none of this.

Instead he sat in the cockpit, taxied along his garden (the lunar rocket was a perfect short strip aircraft) and took off.

The sky was inky, the moon a round, friendly plate, the stars like diamante studs. There was no signpost to tell Captain Colin where to direct his plane, no friendly pit stop in the sky.

It didn't matter. With the instincts of a born pilot, his flight path was strong and true. His hands were on the controls, listening to their every vibration, reading their every signal. He completed a triple loop, laughing in his joy.

Do you remember, reader, that I wrote of a secret in the first chapter of this story? Well, Captain Colin had a secret no longer. He had found his heart and, wherever it took him (or our heart takes us), he knew that its strong and steady beat (and a good compass system) would see him right.

About the Author

AP Whitmore was educated at the University of Bristol, obtaining a BA in French. After working in a variety of roles, she became an independent consultant, in order to focus on her writing. 'The Chronicles of Captain Colin' is her first novel. AP Whitmore lives in Devon.

Lightning Source UK Ltd.
Milton Keynes UK
UKOW04f1818170118
316338UK00001B/11/P